The First Time

by
Stephen J. Burns

WESTVIEW BOOK PUBLISHING, INC.
Nashville, Tennessee

First edition – January 2007

ISBN 1-933912-53-7

Printed in the United States of America on acid-free paper

Edited by Bob Allen and Judy Allen, Author's Corner, LLC

Layout and pre-press by Westview Book Publishing, Inc.

WESTVIEW BOOK PUBLISHING, INC.
PO Box 210183
Nashville, Tennessee 37221
www.westviewpublishing.com

Dedication

I would like to thank my mother and father for their love and support throughout the years and continually encouraging me to live up to my full potential. I also want to thank my three brothers and two sisters for understanding my needs in the face of adversities, such as mental illness.

Stephen J. Burns

For Norma,

The lady that paid me a high compliment – I really appreciate it.

Your friend
Stephen
3/8/07

Foreword

The First Time tells the story of two spirits – the "Earth" and the "Atmosphere" – who discover each other after eons of peace, calm, and loneliness. They quickly learn that their combined powers can create fire, volcanoes, mountains, wind, rain, snow, and hail. As they frolic about reshaping the planet in a newfound friendship, live creatures evolve and establish a food chain in a struggle to become the most superior beings.

Finally, the two spirits through a mediator spirit seek the advice and counsel of the Father on how to keep the most advanced beings from accepting evil and Satan's ways. The Father's guidance and wisdom puts the two spirits at ease with the planet they shaped and challenges them to improve on what they started for the betterment of all beings.

While *The First Time* unfolds references that are remarkably similar to several Biblical stories we have all read and heard, it is purely fictional and conveys a deep passion of love, caring for the well-being of others, and consciously wanting good to triumph over evil. Is *The First Time* a light narrative of our planet's evolution, a love story of spiritual proportions, or purely fantasy? You will have to read the book and make your own decision.

The First Time

"Who is that?"

A pause, long enough to see the sunset, follows before a reply. "I just can't believe we've been here and you've never acknowledged my presence before now. I thought you lacked the ability to respond. Are you stuck in one place or what?"

"Listen! I'm not sure I know what's going on here. All of a sudden after millenniums of being out here all by myself, I find you here. As if the shock of finding you isn't enough, the first thing you have to say to me is that you thought I was too stupid to communicate. That's great! We're off to a really beautiful beginning aren't we now."

"I'm sorry; I don't know what to say."

"Well, I'm sorry too. Why don't we forget it and try to get this ball rolling right?"

"Well, I think it's been rolling right for millenniums as you put it."

"I was talking about the conversation."

"Oh! How do you suppose we can do that?"

"I don't know, but I hope it works out with time."

"Yes, I think a few millenniums of this would be all I could stand."

There was another pause of a few weeks to digest the importance of the last statement.

"I suppose there's a good reason for us being here. I mean, if we weren't supposed to have some type of interaction, we wouldn't be at the same place in the same time, would we?"

"I'd have to think about that. One for you...what types of interaction have you in mind?"

"That's a good one too. I tell you what...why don't we contemplate this for, say...seven years."

"Well really I'm not that slow."

"My dear don't rush the first question you've addressed since we've been here. All we have is time, ourselves, and now each other. These first decisions may be of grave importance. Don't take them lightly."

"Talk to you in seven years."

During this lapse of time both spirits came to the realization that the relation between them could go any of a thousand different directions. The lofty spirit could still taste the arrogance she displayed to her companion and felt remorse for allowing him the upper hand so soon into their relationship. She knew the rules...what type of behavior merited reward. Thus, the decision to back down and allow him the upper hand was the only thing she could do and still remain virtuous. Both of them realized that after eons, they have been given a clean start...a chance to give birth to a planet. A very high honor, it was the aspiration of every spirit to be made something physical in a form that would stem envy or want in other spirits. But this was different. During this seven year prelude, both thought many times how wonderful it was to be one of only two spirits assigned to determine the destiny of an entire planet. Trying to foresee even the slightest change was impossible for them both. The desire to change the planet on its own had never met any success. All that he knew was the perfect symmetry of the center of the planet with its molten core, liquid surface, and the touch of the air of which he could have no part. All she knew were the heights of her bubble which encompassed the water and ice surface which she couldn't penetrate. Their predicaments ensured similar desires in each other...both wanted a tangible piece of each other. He wanted a piece of the sky. She wanted a piece of the earth. The anxiety created by the mere thought of asking the other to give a piece of their domain was great, and neither intended to let their desire be known from the onset. How could they, after such a brash beginning be so impudent with the other? But the interaction...does it have to stay spiritual? What would the consequences be if there were physical interactions? Is the loss of physical matter to the other equated with a loss of spirit? Would the interaction of the two create a third, and would this third also have a separate spirit? Could this spirit be more powerful than either of the two who spawned it?

How could these questions be answered other than by trial and error? And this trial and error process...how could it be contained? There was no way of knowing and the seven years are drawing to a close.

"Hello! Where are you?" she said singing. "I know you're down there somewhere. Seven years have come and gone. Come out! Come out! Wherever you are!"

"That was the shortest seven years I've ever lived through. Have you answered the eternal question?"

"What's that?"

"Is it you or me first?"

"What do you mean?"

"Obviously, either you or I are going to take the lead from here on in."

'Sounds like you have already decided."

"Well I do have a few ideas."

"Slow down buddy-boy I have a few ideas of my own, and I was hoping that we might find some common ground among all these ideas."

"Well maybe you're right. Perhaps the poor first impressions raised a tint of doubt in me. You say you have some ideas."

"Well, during the seven years they must have crossed your mind too. I definitely think we should do some talking before we get started on anything."

"Good idea, we hardly know each other. I was thinking that you may be in the same shape I am. There's no way for me to leave the body of this planet."

"I gave up on that many years ago too."

"Then we're going to be together for some time if not forever."

"Well, long enough that we should find a way to get along together."

"That shouldn't be too hard. If you're worried about those first impressions, don't. I like a spirit with spirit."

"Great! We're on equal ground then?"

"Yes I suppose so."

"This is really good. You seem to be the type of spirit I could get along with for a while."

"Don't forget...we have to. It's going to be a long time."

"Don't you think we should try to get to know each other a little better?"

"I think we should just let it flow and discover each other's idiosyncrasies as they come out."

"OK, I can go along with that. First off though I'd like to tell you I'm jealous of you. I know you are up there closer to the sun and the stars, and all I can do is feel you gliding along my surface. Is it fun?"

"It's not bad, but after all these years it has become routine. I should also confess the jealousy I have for you. You must see and feel the sun and stars. But you also have the center. Is it solid or hollow?"

"It's very hot and liquid in the center. There's also a layer of solid between the liquid surface and molten center."

"That sounds quite nice. Have you ever noticed the way I steal the vapor from your surface to make clouds and rain?"

"You do that?"

"Yes! When I'm bored…which is fairly often?"

"What do you do when you're bored?"

"Well I put a little extra into the waves."

"Does the moon have any affect on you?"

"Yes! It seems to pull at me."

"It pulls at me too! I wonder if it has a spirit."

"I don't know."

"I suppose we'll find out some day. Maybe we should put our efforts together to see if we can do something new."

"I'm game. You have any ideas?"

"Well…what if I try to make a large wave, with the help of brother moon, and you try to pull it up into the sky."

"Sounds pretty tough, but I'll give it a try."

"Here it goes!"

And so, their first cooperative effort was made. It took the better part of several days, but finally the spirit of the air learned to encircle the swell, skimming off the top of the wave, and siphoning the water into clouds, the like of which she had never produced. Such fun was this that it turned into a game to see how many siphons could be maintained like this. The game went on for several years. The spirit of the earth, could at times, feel as though a part of his spirit was raised with the water, and this freedom he enjoyed immensely. The spirit of the sky had never had so much life within her. This honeymoon of circulating the water creating beautiful clouds and terrific rains brought new energy to the two spirits. The excitement of creation, the end of their loneliness, and a future of all sorts of new adventures gave the couple such an exuberant confidence that the eons ahead were bright... something to look forward to. They could not foresee the future, but were anxious to get there.

"That was great!"

"It sure was!"

"You want to do it again?"

"No let's take a break. Let things settle back down to normal."

"OK, I suppose we have plenty of time for that sort of thing. Are you tired?"

"Not really. That picked up my spirits. I just think we ought to do some more talking."

"What do you want to talk about?"

"Well, up till now I've just been calling you "You." Wouldn't you rather have a name more personally suited?"

"Like what? Wait a minute! If you give me a name then I should give you a name."

"I would think it would make things more intimate."

"It should be soft, like you. Simple I suppose, and a little bit feminine."

"Well hurry up. I don't have all day."

"Sure you do."

"OK, I do, but I don't want to spend a lifetime waiting for you to decide what you want to call me."

"We're going to be using these names for a long time. I don't want to get stuck with something I don't like."

"It's easy. Just pick something that comes naturally. It'll be alright. Come on, try me."

"How does Yin sound?"

"Fine, how does Yan sound for you?"

"Hmm, that was simple wasn't it?"

"I'm not trying to push you into anything. If you don't like it say so. We can change it."

"No, I didn't say I didn't like it. It just seems it should be more complicated than that."

"Why?"

"I don't know."

"I have the feeling you worry about things a lot."

"Well, I do like to face a decision with the respect it deserves."

"Is this really such a big deal?"

"I suppose not. Are you happy with your name?"

The First Time

"Say it again."

"Yin."

"I really kind of like it. How do you like Yan?"

"It is very simple."

"I'm glad it's simple. I have this funny feeling you like to complicate things. Maybe this will remind you of how simple things can be."

"OK then. We're agreed on our names. That's it. No more discussion on that then?"

"Yes!"

"Hmm, what do we do next?"

"I don't know. Want to make some more clouds and rain and storms and stuff?"

"No. Let's do something different."

"Like what."

"Maybe we could do the same thing only opposite."

"What do you mean, Yan?"

"If you can pull my water into the air, I should be able to pull your air into my water. Do you mind?"

"No! Go right ahead."

"You let me know if it hurts."

"You're not going to hurt me. Go ahead and try."

"How did you pull me into you?"

"I just kept going around and around the swell till it was sucked up into the clouds."

"Maybe that'll work for me."

"Try it!"

And so he did. With all his might and all the help she could give, he made a whirlpool with the center of air reaching far below his surface. She was full of joy to be finally in the world she could have never before enjoyed. And she did enjoy. Without thinking of consequences, Yan pulled her as deep as he could. What he was not realizing was that, unlike those playful times in the sky, they were actually altering the solid surface beneath the water, creating a crater on the bottom which would not be remedied as easily as letting rain fall to the sea. The symmetry of the sea had never before been shaken. Without realizing it, the two spirits became a couple and took their first step to change the course of their world.

When he finally stopped, he was exhausted. He had never put as much energy into anything before. He was a bit disappointed that he could not handle more than one whirlpool.

Yin realized this and tried to comfort him.

"Water must be so much more difficult to move than air. You should relax. You put a lot of effort into that."

"I was concentrating pretty hard."

"I really enjoyed being down there with you. You know I think I touched bottom a few times."

"It was more than just a few times. We really messed up the surface down there. There's a long crater that I'm not sure I can smooth over. It kind of scares me cause up till now everything was perfectly symmetrical except for when you made clouds and rain and that was temporary. It would be different if we had made a conscious effort, but this was an accident. You don't feel it of course, but I've had currents making their rounds for years. This could upset everything. I can tell already there is a change from the wake as my currents hit this wall. I can feel them come almost all the way to the surface."

"Yan, you're pretty upset about this. Isn't there something you can do? Couldn't you use these currents to smooth it out?"

"I don't think so. It's just like perfection... if you ever lose it you can never get it all back. Even if you get close you still have the memory of being imperfect, which by itself keeps you from being perfect."

"Listen Yan, we know things are going to change and, more likely than not, we won't have control over everything that happens. Just by itself, it shows us that we're not going to have control over everything. We're not going to be able to foresee and control all that happens on this planet. Now things are simple, for as long as we remember being here things have been stable. But you and I know we are older than this planet. We may not remember, but that's because we must concentrate on the physical aspect of being here. We have no need to remember specifics of our life before this. We bring with us the cumulative wisdom of many lives. We have a responsibility to do the best we can with what we have, and I don't think we should shun change. In fact, I feel we have a duty to bring it about...to bring this planet to its full potential. Do you?"

"Well as you said a while back, I think this ball has been rolling right for millenniums, but you do have a point about bringing this planet to its potential. I wonder though... if we keep having these little accidents, aren't we going to eventually lose control over what does and doesn't happen here?"

"The day will probably come when we don't have control over what's important. But don't ever forget that between the two of us we do have control and power to use over this entire planet. We still don't realize the full powers we have. The sky and earth will always be the basic obstacle for anything that wishes to exist here. If there ever comes a time when things get too out of hand we can always use our physical control to stop anything we do not approve of."

"We are just beginning to change this world. I hope we never have to destroy our own work."

"Remember! We just said there is going to be a lot we cannot control."

"Then we must hope for the best?"

"Yes, and never forget who we are."

"I'm really nervous about this lopsidedness. How do we know what's going to happen? The whole planet could get so far out of kilter that it would never produce anything worthwhile."

"Listen! Nothing has happened yet that's hurt anything we would have done with this place. What am I talking about!? We haven't had any plans for this place. All we've done amounts to play. Why are you so worried about a little change? Whatever happens will give us something to start with...whether it is good or bad. Stop fretting about what could happen and try to make what does happen turn into something good."

"OK, but you listen now! Like I said...everything is off balance, and the solid layer between the water and the molten core is shifting. Sooner or later it's going to break and when it does, watch out because the core has terrific pressure. If it gets the chance, it will flow past the water, past you, and all that will be left of our humble abode may be a few meteors in space. Then it will be us trying to explain what we did with our golden opportunity."

"You don't really think that will happen?"

"I think it's a definite possibility."

"I'm sorry."

The First Time

"It's not your fault. It was my idea for the whirlpool."

"I'm still sorry. I have a feeling though that it's not going to be that bad."

"Don't get me wrong. It may not be that bad. I just want to be ready for whatever happens. And if the worse does happen, I want to take responsibility in case there's a second chance. You know there are eight other planets around our star, and if there are other planets forming when this one's blown away I want to be first in line to take over a new one."

"Not a bad contingency plan but let's hope we can salvage this place." "How about controlling the explosion?"

"I'm not sure how that could be done, but it sounds like it may be worth a try. I suppose I could find the weak spots and use another whirlpool to make them weaker. Then we'd know when and where the blow out will come from. There still won't be any containing it once it gets started."

"We're both helpless when it comes to stopping it. But I'd feel much better if it were due to our conscious decision to make it happen."

"We don't have any choice about making it happen. I don't think it would be right to claim it as our own inspiration."

"You never know, it may turn out to be the best thing that could happen."

"Maybe not, but we can say we made the best of the situation."

"You know, in hindsight, this may not amount to much of anything. I really feel like this place is going to go any minute. Are you ready for the big bang?"

"No! Where's the explosion going to be?"

"All along this crater we made."

"Can't you fix it so it'll be all in one place?"

"If you'll stop yakking and help me make another whirlpool to weaken the shell."

"Do it!"

"OK when we get going, we have to stay in one place and bore our way as deep as we can. When it starts to blow just get out of the way and watch or hide. Whatever you do, just don't interfere. Let's get together as soon as we can when it's over."

"OK! Let's go to it!"

Yan tried to imitate what he did to start the first whirlpool, but the crater had changed the currents. It was more difficult to get the spiral started and almost impossible to get the tip to the bottom. At that time he wasn't worried about finding the weakest point, he just wanted to touch bottom and drill as deep as he could in one place. After getting a core started it was easier to stay in one place. After drilling very deep he realized he had made a grave mistake. The shell could not have been as weak as he had originally thought. But now that he had bored so deep, there would be an explosion after all. He knew Yin would not realize what happened; she could not feel the earth. Now he had to decide whether or not to tell her. If he did, she would be on top for never having made such a mistake. If he did not tell her, things would appear as planned, but he would know guilt till the end of time. Perhaps in time the importance of retaining the information would dwindle. A decision such as this could wait, in fact it would have to wait, but for only a while till connotations of fear would become associated with the decision not to come forward with the intimidating situation.

He decided to wait. In fact there would be no time to explain to Yin because the explosion was near. Neither Yan nor Yin could imagine what was about to happen. Yan went quickly to search for Yin. There was little time for conversation and Yan realized this.

"Yin, I don't know what's about to happen, but in case of something catastrophic, know that I will always remember the spirit whose body was pure. I feel that soon you may be subjected to a world very different from what you are accustomed. Bear in mind this is my fault and never forget what you were. I never will."

"Stop making me feel like I'm about to be tortured or something. I know it's going to be different. Is it about to blow or what?"

"Any minute now, I'll talk to you later."

The time had come. Yan was petrified... always thinking of the worst. Yin, the adventurous one, was ready for the fireworks. Both, having always been associated with their own territory, were wary about damage to the domicile they had known for so long and each decided that, whatever happened, their spirit would remain intact to pick up the pieces when it was all over. Neither was prepared for what happened. Yan's early prediction was accurate with the exception of the magnitude of the blast. The spot where he drilled with the whirlpool was the point where the blast originated, but there was such force the perimeter of the hole in the shell was huge.

The molten center found its way to the weakest part and blew a small hole with the contents being thrown with such a force and heat that the water of the sea had no time to cool it. Neither did the atmosphere have the strength to confine it to the planet. The spirits realized what happened and were upset. The planet was all they had and to loose some of it upset them. But there was little time to reflect on that. This reaction continued. Eventually the hole widened, and it seemed as though the entire planet would turn inside out, before it was over. Only the initial blast slung debris into space. When the force was weakened enough to keep the matter inside the confines of the atmosphere the fine matter spread through the skies filling it with clouds of dust, darkening the planet. Eventually the debris, too heavy to stay aloft, began to fall back to the surface around the hole where the blast was still rocketing from the core. This debris sank to the bottom of the sea and built a circular range of mountains which soon displaced the sea. For the first time there was more than water for Yin's bubble to caress. Yan also felt that someday all this turmoil would be worthwhile. The blast continued until the pressure of the core was relieved and the temperature of the blasted material began to equalize with the temperature of the sea, the atmosphere, and the shell which remained intact.

But it seemed as if it would never stop. The range of mountains formed by the debris was eventually filled with molten debris. When the massive rock was developed into one huge mountain the pressure from beneath cracked it. The crater which Yin and Yan created cracked open and again the inside of the planet spewed forth to form additional mountain ranges.

This whole series of events took years and years to pass. When everything quieted down for the most part, the two spirits began to search for one another. During the period in which both the spirits had their domains changed so radically they both thought to themselves of the time in the beginning when everything was pure, symmetrical, uneventful, and quiet. Reflecting on that time was to ensure a memory; perhaps to set a goal for a time or situation in the future. Both thought that it would be a long time in coming even if there was to be a time to resemble the age of perfect order. Whatever was to come, it would be the first step into a seemingly endless pursuit. With the knowledge that it would take cooperation between the spirits, the search for each other did not take long.

"Well why don't we try that on the other side? This lopsidedness makes me dizzy."

"Are you sure you haven't always been a little dizzy?"

"I'm serious!"

"No sir! We're not going to do it again on the other side. I've got a whole layer of soot, higher than any cloud has ever gone, the sun rays are blocked and I feel nasty! Not to mention this big lump of you protruding into my bubble. Believe you me... if I ever figure out how to get my territory back into a decent state I'm not even

[15]

going to consult you. How are we ever going to make something out of this mess? The temperature has dropped, the whole order of things has changed and you want to straighten out the lopsidedness by doing it all over again on the other side. I don't know about you Yan. I'm beginning to think I'm going to be stuck here for an eternity with a dim wit."

"There you go again! Not five minutes are we together and you've insulted me again. What's so wrong about wanting my territory to be balanced?"

"You'll never get it balanced the way it was in the beginning, so forget about that will you? And I'm sorry for calling you a dim wit. I'm just upset a little from losing the peace and quiet we used to have."

"Well it's OK. Stop worrying. Everything will turn out alright someday."

"That someday may be a long time from now."

"I know. Just try to bear it the best you can."

"Well we have a bit different situation to work with now. I have a feeling there will be more to do than just to make water spouts and whirlpools. This ash is blocking the sun...can you feel a difference?"

"Yes! The water is where I feel the temperature change the most. Of course the poles are always cold as usual. I'm not really concerned too much about the temperature change. The things I'm worried about are the things you can't feel. The whole mass of me is churning up. The shell is weakening in several places and I'm beginning to feel there is no way for me to stop it now."

"In short, you're about to explode into me again."

"You know I'd stop it if I could, but I can't. Everything is changing down here. I don't feel I'm losing control, but that I'm just beginning to learn how to control things here."

"Well if you're trying to learn how to control things you better get back to it. You know, what we're learning now may be the only tools we have to control whatever does become of this planet. Other than wind and rain I don't have anything to work with. Perhaps the layer of soot you presented me with could be used for something. I'll try to see what I can possibly use it for while you learn your lessons in the sphere. Don't feel bad about whatever you do with the planet. Right now it's just us against it. There's really no reason to be gentle with it."

"Then you don't mind if there are some more explosions?"

"No. Don't try to avoid that because of me. I'm sure I'll find a use for this solid stuff somehow."

"Well that's a relief, because I'm fixing to blow in several places. I'm glad you're relaxed about this. I don't know if I could have held it back."

"Now again… if you could learn how to hold it back, it may become quite useful in bringing some order to the planet when needed. But, for now, I suppose it won't hurt to let you bubble up into me a few times.

"Thanks Yin. I knew you weren't the stereotypical feminine spirit. I have a feeling you're going to be nice to have as a partner."

"Don't count your blessings before they've come to pass."

"Oh no, did I blow it?"

"No. But get back to business."

"Talk to you when I get this ball under control."

"Learn your tricks well!"

The First Time

"You too!"

"Bye!"

Yan went straight to work. The first thing was to determine where the weakest part of the shell was. It appeared to be on the opposite side of the planet from the first blast. He wasn't really dizzy from the lopsidedness, but wanted to bring back the symmetry. He realized fully that the blissful symmetry he once knew was lost forever. Little did he realize that there was more to "balance" than perfect physical symmetry. Yan allowed some of the tension in the shell to relieve itself using close to the same techniques he used the first time. However, he strained to be aware of all the pressures in all the dimensions of the sphere. Never before was he able to know the planet as he did now. Everywhere in the planet there were tensions waiting to be relieved. Yan learned that everywhere he caused an action, a reaction was felt somewhere else. For what turned out to be hundreds of years, he battled to find stability. During these years he never sought Yin's company because of his terrific guilt that the situation was his fault. He would not see her until he had at least stabilized the situation and learned how to master the territory of which he was supposed to be master.

Yin was lonely. For those hundred's of years, which to her were not such a relatively long time, she had little to do. Of course Yan's new explosions added more to the "layer of soot" in her upper atmosphere. But the soot was broken into such small particles it would eventually become less of a screen from the sunlight and more of a filter. Yin felt good about this. As usual, she felt it would serve a good purpose someday.

As Yan asked her to do, she mastered her tricks too, learning to make water spouts by herself, simple rain, and by accident, something new, hail. She had always been content with soaking up water until the clouds wanted to fall, and so, she let them fall. But for some unrecognized reason one day she said no. As the rain began to fall she said "No" and made a wind to carry the drops back up high into the clouds. After having done this several times, she allowed the drops to fall, and after they had fallen to the sea, she saw that they were round balls of ice. Ice just like Yan's poles were made of. "Pretty neat little trick!" she thought.

Of course the best toy for her to play with was the land left from the explosions Yan allowed. She studied how the waves would batter the shores of the islands and wash away a little with each stroke. She thought she too should be able to alter them if she could gather enough force. And this she tried. Rains, just as strong as any she had ever provided. But she was disappointed. It was either not strong enough or didn't last long enough to produce much of an effect. Then she tried hail, but that didn't do much better. She would like to be able to wash the whole mound away, but soon realized that the mass would be there a long time. Only after years and years of constant rain would she have much success. It was no big loss. She realized things had changed. But, just like Yan, she would have preferred to put things back the way they were for so many years.

Even at that, all her effort was not in vain. She observed she did have some effect on the mass. In some places she formed pools of water. The mirroring pools reminded her of her partner though, and she often wondered if Yan had had time to notice them. She thought it would be nice for him to have a more confined, but familiar place other than the water for them to get together. Perhaps someday there would be a useful purpose for the pool. Everyday she thought of that someday to come. It made her anxious to have her partner find out what his "someday" held.

It wasn't long before Yan worked things out to where everything was relatively stable. At least stable enough to where he could have the time to be with Yin without a major happening in the shell. At this point he realized that there would never be a time when there wasn't tension somewhere. He also felt he did not owe his soul to the planet as mediator among forces. That could actually be left to the planet itself. He no longer felt that it was his responsibility to promote or oversee every shift and eruption. Finally, after years of self debate, he decided it wasn't his entire fault. The symmetry was shaken by accident. Sooner or later the shell would have responded. No longer did the guilt force him into making amends by trying to control the course that nature would invoke one way or another. The freedom of this guilt and the years of diligent work trying to get to know his tricks or territory, which he learned quite well, spurred in him the confidence he needed to face his partner. So that was what he did.

It did not take long to find her. When he did, things went so well it was as if they may have been separated for only a day instead of over a hundred years.

"Yan! Do you know what you're doing down there now?"

"Sure I do! Watch this mountain here," and Yan blew up the mountain with a conservative eruption, then stopped the flow of lava leaving a crater of bubbling hot rock. "Beat that!"

"Well, I may not be able to beat that, but watch this!" And so Yin took a clear sky and filled it with clouds using a huge water spout. Then churning up as much hail as she thought appropriate for the situation, she delivered hail, torrential rains, and winds to the crater, cooling the pool of molten rock and leaving in its place a serene pool. Yan was quite impressed ... just as impressed was Yin with Yan."

"You've learned some neat tricks!"

"You too!"

Before the couple had a chance to further the conversation, something happened that shocked them both ... literally. A bolt of lightning, originating in the newly formed pool, jumped in an arc to some clouds which Yin left hovering to give her territory a more tactile quality. Yin suspected Yan of having learned more than he was letting on. Yan thought the same thing. Yan spoke first. "Now that's one hell of a trick!"

"I know. How did you do it?"

"I didn't do it … you did it, didn't you?"

"No, I didn't do it. Don't be fooling around with me Yan. That's pretty awesome stuff you've gotten a hold on."

"Listen, I'm not teasing. I didn't do that. Not that I wouldn't like to know how, but I just didn't do it!"

"I can't believe we've spent over a hundred years learning our tricks, and now when we finally get together we're dumbfounded with something we know nothing about, have never witnessed before, and is so powerful we both probably consider the ultimate interplanetary phenomena."

"Wait a minute! Are you sure you want to label it the "ultimate?"

"Well, I don't know about you, but I got the best jolt I've ever had from it."

"That's fine for you, but all I felt was a bit of the energy in me being tapped and transferred to you."

"Well it felt terrific to me!"

"What did you do with it?"

"I just soaked it up. It really did feel good. I haven't felt this good in years. It went way up inside me, filled me with energy, then dispersed and flowed into me. You've got to do that again!"

"I'm not sure, but I think this has to be done on a cooperative basis. I'll offer you a little bit of energy, but you're going to have to coax it out of me."

"Fine, let's do it!"

"Wait a minute would you? I think this is something you don't want to rush!"

"Sure it is! Do it again!"

"I just said I thought it took some cooperation."

"Well what do you want me to do?"

"I don't know! It only happened once."

"Well hurry up."

"If you're in such a rush, why don't you do it by yourself?"

"How?"

"Damn girl! I don't know how to do it with the both of us. Not to mention doing it by myself."

"Well I'm sorry, but we've got to figure this out soon. That beats rain, wind, and water spouts altogether."

"Let's be rational about this and maybe we will figure it out. But if it takes as much out of me as it did that first time, and you like it as much as you say, I may regret this."

"Don't worry! I'll take it easy on you. Please! Just once more and I'll leave you alone."

"I don't want you to leave me alone. I want you to remember it's been over a hundred years since I've been with you and I do not want to be overcome with a new trick."

"That was one nice trick."

"We'll figure it out. Like I said, it felt to me like energy flowing from me into you."

"I wasn't trying to get it from you; I was just showing my stuff then... whammy."

"Show me your "stuff" again."

"With pleasure, what would you like me to do?"

"I'm going to stay here on this island, so why don't you just get together as much rain and wind as you can muster."

"Fine."

And rain it did for days. Yan wasn't sure how to do the trick but he surely enjoyed the wind and rain… just like the good ole days.

"OK. It's been raining for days. Where's my jolt?"

"You're ready for this... huh?"

"Yes." "OK. I don't think I can stand much more rain. Now remember... you've got to want it as much as I want to give it."

"I want it."

"OK. Here it comes." With all his might, Yan summoned as much energy as he could to the point in the pool where the first jolt came from. There were still ominous clouds in the sky. Yan warned Yin, and then let it flow. Not just one jolt but an entire evening of one jolt after another. Yin was delirious. The energy flowed through her entire territory, forcing her to the point where she had to ask Yan to stop.

"If I didn't think it was close to sinful, I'd want you to do that all day tomorrow, the next day, and on into next week! Don't ever forget that trick!"

"Don't ever stop coaxing it out of me."

"I'm tingling all over. Especially, in the deeper reaches of my space."

"Well I wish I could say it's had the same effect on me, but actually

I'm a little tired… sort of drained."

"I'm sorry, but thank you. Is there anything I can do for you?"

"How about giving me a day of clear skies so I can soak up some rays?"

"You've noticed this layer of soot is filtering out the sun haven't you?

"No I haven't taken the time to notice actually."

"It's pretty thick, but dissipates after the fireworks are over, for the most part anyway."

"I'm fairly sure there won't be any eruptions for a while now."

"Good! I'll give you a few days of the most beautiful skies you've ever seen. Actually you'll like this layer of particles. It works like a filter and takes the bite out of the sun's rays."

"Are you sure all that energy you just soaked up hasn't?..."

"Hasn't what? Made me a little crazy? Sure it has! And it should! I've been sitting around here for hundreds of years with nothing to do, and no one to talk to. Then you pull the best trick ever and I'm not supposed to 'go a little crazy?' I'm not a rock you know. I need a diversion every once in awhile."

"You liked that diversion didn't you?"

"It's the next best thing to heaven."

"Don't bring heaven into this. We're going to be here one long time."

"Sorry."

"It's OK."

"Can we do it again?"

"Yes, maybe in a week or two."

Why so long?"

"Sounds like I found a weakness."

"Weakness!"

"Sure! If you can't last a week without it wouldn't you call it a weakness?"

"No. I'd just say I want a little more of a good thing."

"Fine, we'll give it a go again tonight then forget about it for another hundred years or so."

"Yan...you've found my weakness."

"Good, how about some blue skies?"

"We don't have to avoid it then?"

"No."

"Good. Did you want some wind with those blue skies?"

"Why not, you always did rub me the right way."

"What do you want to do with this place? I mean everything we've done so far has been accidental; what do you want to do purposefully?"

"I don't think I know all my options. As a matter of fact, I don't recall ever having an option in advance. You know, I want everything to turn out to be a credit in the Father's eyes. I think we have a long way to go, but I can tell you're one who would rather serve than be served. That's admirable. I hope we never have a conflict concerning a decision of propriety. You know, a lot could happen on this planet. I hope we never lose "touch" with one another. Now it's just you and me, and I'll never forget the times we've had so far, but let me say right now, we know we'll be around to the end unless the end is the annihilation of the planet. God save us if we should permit any type of life form to destroy our own abode. Speaking of life forms, how would you feel about life forms on our planet?"

"Well, you know the Father does not approve of just any old type of life form. What type of life form did you have in mind?"

"As far as that's concerned, I think I'll just sit back and hope for the best. Do you think that's a safe approach?"

"Like I say, the Father doesn't approve of all life forms."

"I was thinking I could wait until things started to get out of hand."

"I think you'd be taking a real chance. There's little to say to a life form trying to carry on. What would make you think that you, a spirit, would be able to step in and curtail the existence of a life form firmly established?"

"I figured you'd be with me on any decision like that, and that the two of us together, would be invincible if need be."

"Well maybe we would. I just wish we had some type of life form to give our attention to."

"Well, my dear, I have a surprise for you. You remember the night we discovered lightning?"

"Yes."

"Well, besides just having a good time ourselves, we discovered something else. All of that "soot" as you called it was charged with the lightning. Subsequently, some of this supercharged "soot" fell to the sea where some wonderful metamorphosis took place so that now we have a good "stand" of super green soot which grows and grows because there is nothing to stop it. I foresee perhaps three years before it leaves the confinement of water and "takes over" on land too."

"This is not good. How are we going to stop it?"

"Well rain, hail, wind, and lightning won't stop it. Neither will volcanoes and earthquakes."

"Have we already lost control?"

"We lost control the first time we had a whirlpool."

"Then we can't stop it."

"Why would we want to stop it?"

"Is it acceptable to the Father?"

"I don't know."

"I wish we could get some type of communication with them. If it isn't acceptable we might get some type of divine intervention and learn what to do with ourselves!"

"I haven't had any contact with the Father since I've been here. Have you?"

"No."

"Then what makes you think we would be given an audience now?"

"I don't know, but I would like some type of guidance in this. We're in the beginning of life for this planet and if we do allow an unacceptable life form to evolve here, we will loose grace with the Father. And I don't want that."

I have a feeling we're supposed to do the best we can without divine guidance."

"You don't want divine intervention?"

"It's not that I don't want it. It's just that they obviously don't want us contacting them. They would have given us an idea of how to contact them if it were going to work that way. I truly feel they want us to do the best we can first."

"OK then. We go it alone. What do we do with this green stuff that's taking over everything?"

"We let it take over everything."

"It's that simple!"

"I remember you once said that you thought I was the one to make everything so complicated?"

"You mean we're just going to stay out of it and let this stuff grow?"

"Yes."

"I feel helpless."

"Get used to it."

"I think I'm going to conjure up a storm. Care to join me?"

"Why not, you know I really enjoy the way you do me."

"Think you could work up some lightning for me?"

"And start up a new batch of green stuff?"

"Damn. I forgot about that."

"Listen! Don't worry about it."

"Are you serious?"

"Sure!"

"We're going to end up in hell."

"No we're not."

"Yes we are. You just wait and see!"

"The day will come when we get our just reward."

"Just reward for allowing this planet to be taken over by condemned life forms, while we play with our powers to simply entertain ourselves."

"Do you really think the Father expects us to be all work and no play with this planet? This place is us. We have all the time in the world. Why should we be worried about this green stuff? We know right and wrong. Relax a bit, would you?"

"OK, but I'm going to keep a watch on that stuff."

Years went by, and the green stuff did spread, filling the oceans deep and wide, washing ashore to anchor itself upon the miles of lava. Everywhere it could survive, and there were only a few places, such as the poles and active volcanoes, where it couldn't spread. It came to a point when there was no more room. It crowded itself so much, that in some places, it fell back on itself helplessly. It died, rotted, and caused a new metamorphosis. A new, more complex type of life form was created."

Yan said: "Have you noticed this new stuff consuming the green stuff?"

"Yan, it is feeding on the green stuff."

"So!"

"You don't realize what's happened!"

"It's no big deal…we're finally going to clean up the green stuff."

The First Time

"Yan, I thought you realized…any life form that must take life from another life form in order to survive is automatically condemned for taking life."

"Would you really call what this stuff is a life form?"

"It's one of the simplest forms, yes, it is a life form."

"Well, if it's so simple, what are you upset about?"

"You think simple life forms don't come into play when figuring the worth of life forms."

"I'm sure there will be more complex and worthy life forms to live on this planet. At least I hope there will be."

"Yan, you're overlooking something."

"What?"

"If you allow the destruction of one of the simplest life forms, you would probably not stop there."

"Well, I don't know what you're getting at."

"If you allow the destruction of simple life forms, you would probably allow the destruction of the even simpler forms of life."

"Meaning?"

"God save me! You idiot! That's us!"

"Oh!"

"Oh, is right!"

"Calm down! Listen! Everything is going to be alright. Tell me…did you ever hear of a life form that didn't feed on another, other than a spirit or an inanimate form?"

"No, but I'm not omnipotent either."

"I don't think such a thing exists."

"I would feel a lot better if it did."

"You're condemning yourself before you know how the Father would really feel about this. It could be that they would commend us for somehow producing a life form. It may be that the spirits inhabiting other planets which haven't produced any life forms are on a lower stage than we are on."

"You really think so?"

"I think it's a good possibility."

"I'd feel better if they sent us approval about what's happened."

"We're one of billions of planets and we have little to show so far. I'd feel foolish to request an audience without something more to show."

"Then you think we should allow this stuff to find its own path?"

"Yes…to the point where the Father asks us to step in and alter the course."

"Then what's next?"

"Well, I'm not sure, but in the places the green stuff is being eaten, it seems as though it is taking on qualities to combat the bacteria…strong plants, more resistant. Have you noticed the way some of it on land is trying to rise up off the rocks so it won't be eaten?"

"Well, that beats all. I never noticed."

"You can't see it, but down below the green stuff, it is forming hundreds of different types of species. But for every one that develops putting a new type of bacteria out of business, sooner or later a more complex form is evolved, designed specifically to feed on the plant which had just changed to evade the bacteria."

"What are these bacteria like?"

"Every time it reproduces, it changes, or so it seems. I haven't, and don't intend to keep tabs on it, but I must confess right now that as far as I'm concerned, the more complex it gets, the better off we are. I'm sure it will take many years before this process of evolution produces a life form impressive enough to present to the Father. So, the sooner it does, the better."

"What do we do in the mean time?"

"There's this little island close to the south pole. It's going to be very boring around here for the next few thousands of years, so how would you feel about setting up shop on the island for a while? We wouldn't be tempted to meddle with the evolution, and we could lose ourselves in ourselves for a while."

"You mean not even bother with keeping up with the world?"

"We could check on things every once in a while, but I would rather just let it go, then come home to whatever has happened."

"You know if we don't take responsibility for this mess, we may not get the credit either."

"I'm not worried about that. We started it, even if by accident. We allowed it to carry on. How could we lose credit for it? Besides, if we don't take advantage of this free time now, we may never get another chance."

"OK. Let's go. Where exactly is this place now?"

"South, almost to the ice cap, tall mountains, you can't miss it. There's a volcano keeping the life away."

"Sounds nice."

"Supercharged for your electrical pleasures."

"I'm going to give you a storm to make your lava pits sizzle."

"You're going to get it."

"All talk and no action."

"Race you!"

The couple relished the time they took off from the world, which was beginning to worry them. Turning their back was not as easy as they had indicated to each other. Yan's apparent boldness was a front for Yin's benefit. Yin, seeing through it, privately housed the fear associated with collusion with Yan. She knew there would not be a way to stop it now...the chain had started. Pointing it out to the Father and asking for help, would possibly end the chance she knew was a blessing. Her "someday" now, held hopes for nothing more than a time when the end of the "chain" would be found and an end to the fight for survival would be realized. The future held "someday," memories that were a time of quiet solitude. She was grateful of Yan's suggestion to leave the infancy of the chain to the laws which would govern it until the time the life it would produce, would choose to end the chain itself. These were matters she knew the Father would certainly enter into, but for now, she agreed with Yan, there was little that could be done to stop the horror, little to show the Father for the gift He bestowed them.

Yan somehow realized all this too, but for him there was resolve...a determination to see through the troubles and detach himself from them. Putting himself in a place of refuge was a natural, easy thing to do. He would have found an escape for himself easily and without guilt...just as he escaped the guilt of allowing the disturbance. Yin felt this in Yan, but she also felt a sincere compassion. The compassion was evidenced by his treatment of Yin. He knew she would not be able to put things in the same perspective as he, so he took her to a place he hoped he could spare her the gruesomeness they both accidentally unleashed.

The race did not take long, but the fireworks didn't start immediately. They knew each other too well to ignore their mixed emotions. There was so much to communicate, yet not a word said until they realized the best thing to do was to carry on with the plan.

"This is a nice little island! How come I never noticed it before?"

"I just made it yesterday."

"Did you really?"

"Yes."

"Keep this up and I may start loving you."

"I didn't think you would be that easy."

"I'm not easy."

"I know."

"Are you easy?"

"Yes! Or at least I try to be."

"Are you saying what I think you are trying to say?"

"Yes."

"Well why don't you say it?"

"You're doing a pretty good job of it for me."

"Yan, this is not fun."

"Do you really want it to be fun when I do say what you think I want to say?"

"It wouldn't hurt. It hurts to wait to hear you say it."

"We have all day."

"I'm about to cry so hard it will put out your volcano."

"Don't do that. I wish I knew how this stupid conversation got started. I go to all this trouble to make this island, get you to forget your troubles, all just so I could tell you "I love you", and you're about to cry."

"You said it."

"What?"

"Oh damn you Yan!"

"I swear you make me so confused I don't know if I'm here or there!"

"You are right here and you just said it."

"I haven't been able to say anything!"

"Oh yes you have!"

"I think I'd better shut up."

"If you know what's good for you, you'd better start all over, and slowly and distinctly, say what's on your mind."

"OK. Slowly and distinctly…you are the most confusing entity in God's universe!"

"I can not believe it. Do you love me?"

"Five minutes ago I did."

"I'm getting sick."

"Yin, I don't know how this got started, but all of a sudden, after years of being without you, and looking forward to the day that I could tell you how I feel, I find myself feeling totally helpless. I planned out every word. Now look at us. I'm about to lose control of this volcano and you're sick."

"Maybe this can wait."

"No! It can't!"

"Then say it."

"What?"

"You love me!"

"It's not that simple."

"Well Yin I know what I want to say, but I just can't say it anymore. I had it all figured out. But now, after all this..."

"Yan, three words ... I love you."

"Thank you. I love you too. Now did you have something else to say?"

"Yep, But they won't come out the way I wanted them to."

"Why?"

"Cause we're both upset."

"You know what?"

"What."

"As hard as it was to get you to say those three words, I don't think I would have had it any other way. I'll never forget the last five minutes."

"Yin, do you love me?"

"Yes"

"Would you let me try that again?"

"Please do."

"I don't mean right now."

"Anytime."

"Yin?"

"Hmm."

"I love you."

"I love you, too."

The mood created by the dialogue between the two spirits lasted the duration of their stay on the island. Both felt that for some reason, things could never be perfect. Despite the good times and triumphs of mastering their territories, the stigma associated with the bad luck from the beginning of their relationship seemed to put a damper on everything. There was a cloud over their avowed love. Even the simple pleasure of acknowledging their love carried with it the obligation to admit fault with the situation. Both of them inwardly verified the innocence of their partner, yet the inability to escape the situation nullified the attempt to free them from the stigma. They knew the waiting game had just started. There was little said about the future even though this was paramount in their minds. There was little desire for the innocent play they once lost themselves in. There were awkward times of prolonged silence. During these times though, both tried to think to the future trying to see past the early stages of the troubles. This thought process reversed itself though. Both struggled to remember the time before they met and even further back. Where did they come from? What was before they came to the planet? How the presence of the Father known...there was no recollection of any interaction with Him. Both of the spirits possessed simple wisdom. How? There was something there in a dark past. Would they ever know? After a while curiosity took over. Yin was curious, but scared. Yan, knowing this, decided to explore the situation for them both.

"I want an accurate report."

"Don't worry. I won't spare you any of the gory details."

"Come on."

"Whatever's going on, we're not to interrupt it."

"I still want to know."

"Trust me. I'll let you know anything you should know."

"Don't let it eat you."

"I'm a spirit."

"Oh yeah! I forgot."

"You know, when I concentrate I can feel what they're doing with the planet."

"Does it hurt?"

"No, it's strange. I can feel the life taking its substance from me, but the life itself, is not really a part of me."

"Oh no! There are already independent life forms developing."

"I don't know. There's none around here. I'll be back before the sun sets."

"Be careful."

"There's nothing dangerous."

"How do you know?"

"I just do. Bye!"

"Bye."

It didn't take long for Yan to verify his suspicions. In these years of waiting, there were considerable advances in the food chain. The simple bacteria that fed on algae when they retreated to the island were now the prey of larger more complicated organisms. Yan was never concerned with the primitive forms of life. They were just natural occurrences...progressions that evolved from occurrences in the physical realm, but more complicated forms were striving for more than substance to survive. They were striving to expand their ability to sense the tangible aspects of the planet. By mere observation, Yan could tell the most complex of these organisms had the ability to sense movement through the water, change in their environment such a temperature, but perhaps most importantly, were the abilities they used to sense each other and live as a group. Even though they were independent from each other, they stayed together seeking the substance to survive. They depended on each other to seek out the lower forms of life from which they spawned themselves. Yan knew though, that each time a newer generation came forth there was a difference, which was the ability desired by the predecessor to overcome any obstacles. Yan wondered how many generations it would take before all obstacles, presented by the planet he and Yin commanded, were overcome; at what point would this life be able to support its needs long enough to realize the challenges that lay before them in order for them to become a permanent presence in a world the Father would allow to exist.

Having satisfied his curiosity, Yan left the area to return to the refuge of the island. During the short time it took him to relocate he thought to himself of the past. In just a brief interlude, he recalled the highlights of his time in the planet. Everything from the time before Yin, up to the present, could be recalled in only a few minutes. This caused him to believe that this must only be the beginning. The problem was the recollection of the unhappy times. It spurred in him feelings of great anxiety. If such a long length of time held so many problems, what was there to be in the future? When would the "someday," he and Yin always spoke of, come to be? The anxiety associated with the contemplation of the future caused Yan to confront the situation he had to deal with. Soon he would be back with Yin and her thousand questions. What would he say? How would he ever get her through the eons of pain? And, for the first time he felt a desire to have the Father to step in to somehow ease the burden the spirits carried.

"Well, welcome back!"

"Thanks! Have you been alright since I've been gone?"

"Oh, just a little bit lonely."

"I wasn't gone that long was I?"

"You were gone long enough for me to miss you?"

"In a way I'm glad you missed me."

"What do you mean, in a way?"

"Oh, nothing. I just hoped you'd be able to occupy yourself while I was gone."

"Oh, I did!"

"What did you do?"

"I decided to leave our humble abode and see what was going on."

"Oh really! Then you shouldn't have missed me at all."

"It took me almost no time to see enough to thoroughly disgust me enough that I raced back here and waited for you."

"You think it's that bad?"

"It is the worst of all possible worlds."

"Don't get so upset. There's nothing we can do about it. We've discussed this before."

"When?"

"I don't know, but you realized that we can't stop it. We'll have to let these life forms progress into something with the intelligence to survive in a manner that the Father will accept."

"But what do we do when the Father comes and asks what we're doing about this?"

"We simply ask Him to allow them to progress into a form He might accept."

"And what if He says no?"

"We do whatever they ask us to. But they can't say we didn't try."

"I think we should stop this mess now."

"Then what?"

"I don't know, but I'm afraid to let something He couldn't accept go on."

"You're not the Father and you don't know what they will and won't accept. What's going on out there now is life without choice. Survival is the only thing. I'm not so sure the Father wouldn't be very pleased with this."

"Don't be ridiculous."

"I don't think I'm being ridiculous."

"Then I suppose we'll have to wait for the Father."

"Wait if you want to. I hope He doesn't show up until this evolution produces something we can be proud of."

"I couldn't ever be proud of anything that comes out of this mess."

"Yin, promise me something."

"What?"

"That you won't put an end to this if you get the chance. Wait until the Father says to do it."

"If I knew another way to bring life to this planet, I wouldn't make that promise, but since I don't, you have my word."

"Thank you."

"So what do we do to speed up this process?"

"There's nothing we can do. Just wait."

"How long?"

"I don't know. It could take eons."

"Oh really! And what do you suggest we do in the meantime?"

"Ignore what's been going on and do the same thing we did for the eons before we met."

"I can't do that. My existence in that state was interrupted. I'll never be able to have the same peace I had then. What about you? Do you want to revert into the planet and forget about me?"

"No, not at all. I love you. I hate the thought of being without you. It's just that somehow we must get through this period. You don't appear to be able to accept what is going to happen. So I'm suggesting that we spend this time in solitude, detached from the planet and the life it's creating. It just seems that would be the easiest way to do it."

"Maybe you're right, but I don't think I want to go into hibernation just yet.

"I don't either. Let's decide what we would like to do before we go docile, do it, then go into our sleep."

"That sounds good. What would you like to do?"

"Everything we can without interrupting the life."

"Such as?"

"Stick you with the most powerful bolt of lightning you've ever imagined."

"You really get a jolt out of that, don't you?"

"Yes."

"If the memory of this is to last eons, you must really put yourself out for it."

"I will! But don't forget that you're the one who must conjure it out of me."

"I know it's been a while, but I haven't lost my stuff. Tell me something. Do you think we should hang on to this island as our rendezvous?"

"No. It takes too much concentration to control this volcano."

"Remember when I said I was going to make your lava pits sizzle?"

"Vaguely."

"Well I'm going to."

"Very interesting. Do you have any idea how much water it would take to do that?"

"Quite a bit."

"Do you know what it would feel like to center myself in the volcano and have you douse me completely?"

"No, and never will, but hopefully it would be nice enough to provoke a response suitable for a memory to last eons."

"Probably would."

"Get ready lover, because here it comes." And at that instant Yin blew hard and deep into the surface causing a tidal wave that snuffed the fiery crater. Yan was shocked as he wasn't expecting such a sudden display of power. The first thing that came to mind was the surprise in Yin's ability. He never saw her use such an awesome amount of energy. Then the sensation of instantaneous relief, all fire seeks, put her in a different light. The light only the most feminine of females can provoke. Then it happened. From the inner most region of the sphere energy, even Yan didn't know was available, summoned itself below the crater, held back with all Yan's might until it was no use. It rocketed through the surface creating a temporary bond between the center of the planet and the upper reaches of the atmosphere. For just a moment Yan and Yin could sense the dimensions of the entire planet, more vivid and complete than either had ever dreamed of. A frozen instant of life each gave another never to be forgotten.

"I think that will get me through a few eons."

"Yes. I think that will last me awhile too. In fact I don't think I could handle doing that again before a few eons."

"I'll still miss you."

"I'll miss you too, but I think I can make it now."

"Where are you going to locate yourself during the sabbatical?"

"I will be between the moon and the planet. I think that will be an easy place to stay. Just concentrating on the easy pull will let me sleep peacefully."

"I think I'll make a lake with no life and sleep until life wakes me."

"Sounds good. Would you wake me after you're awakened?"

"Sure I think that's a good plan. That way we don't have to bother checking the life until it's able to cause some type of commotion."

"Maybe we should check on it."

"Leave it to me. I'll wake you when it's time."

"Good bye! I love you."

"I love you."

"Promise not to dream of anyone but me."

"I don't know anyone but you."

"Good. Don't dream up anyone."

"Eons are a long time Yin."

"I know. Can I trust you?"

"Yes. Can I trust you?"

"Yes."

"Good bye."

"Good bye."

And so began a period in the history of the planet which was all but forgotten. For the two spirits, it was time suspended to allow, what was in their eyes, a time of necessary evil. However it was viewed, it was a time of slow unrelenting pain for the life involved with it. Survival was the solitary issue. All life during this time faced one problem...its position in the food chain, what to consume and what to be consumed by. The latter half of the issue, a concept of simple horrifying realities, was the driving force behind the process of evolution. The constant question in all life was how to escape being consumed. Of course this led to larger more sensually aware creatures. The facts of life during this time would not allow a species to remain unchanged, that would only allow the species to fall prey to another species knowledgeable of consistent weakness. So on top of not knowing peace due to the awareness of its place in the food chain there was also the despair of knowing that life for any one particular species was only a temporary privilege. Coupled with this however, was the hope that one day the pain in existence would be over and that a life form would evolve that would not have to exist in a constant state of fear and anxiety that its physical attributes could be overcome by another form of life. Also this ultimate form of life would have the peace associated with the lack of striving to evolve into a more dominant species, thus allowing for the first time, pursuit of more noble endeavors.

This process went on for eons with the spirits in a state of content recluse. Yan made his relocation in the center crater of five volcanoes. The four on the outside of the center were off shoots of the center. The center had gone dormant and filled with water. The heat prevented any algae from starting there and he knew the outlying volcanoes would provide a clock for him...when those volcanoes became dormant, life would creep in and allow the decedents of the algae and bacteria to disturb him. This happened.

"What in the world is going on here?"

There were three huge dinosaurs feasting on the plant life close to the lake.

"Well I'll be damned! It worked! Look at the size of those things. Now, that you can present to the Father! I've got to find Yin."

It was as if a miracle happened overnight to Yan. In the brief survey he made on the way to the other side of the planet where Yin and the moon were, Yan concluded his plan had worked. Everywhere there were signs of life. He did not take the time to examine it, but felt pleased there had been so much progress.

"Yin! Are you here? Wake up!"

"OK, OK. What's going on?"

"They did it. You should see...creatures of every shape and size! Come on and see!"

"Take it easy. Don't rush me. How long have we been asleep?"

"I don't know. Long enough for some of the strangest life forms you've ever seen to evolve."

"Are they still consuming each other?"

"Well sure. But what did you expect for such a few years?"

"A few years … I thought we'd been dormant for eons."

"I don't know or care how long it took. We did it! We have to get the Father here to check this out."

"If they're still consuming life, he is not going to like it."

"It's our best try. Come on! See for yourself!"

"OK. You lead, I'll follow. How long have you been awake?"

"Just for a little while. I was awakened by three huge beasts eating the plants in my lake."

"A beast eating plant life?"

"Yes."

"Well maybe that's not as bad as a beast eating a beast."

"They're on the other side of the planet. Let's go."

Yan couldn't contain his jubilance. Yin, as usual, was cynical. But they did take a while to discuss the situation.

"Things have only gotten worse."

"Why do you say that?"

"Because it is true ... they eat each other. They're no better than the bacteria and algae. They have nothing except survival in their heads."

"Well I'm satisfied now. You can call in the Father to get approval or suggestions, whatever."

"You don't want any more time?"

"No. I think it's gone far enough."

"I'm not sure I know how to get the Father here."

"I was thinking He might show up by himself."

"When was the last time you had any dealings with the Father?"

"I really don't remember, but it must have been when He sent me here."

"I don't remember either. You know I don't have a clear memory of anything before the dormant time, before we found each other."

"This is great. We finally have something to show Him and we don't know how to get Him here. For some reason, I want to say He is omnipresent."

"Me too. Do you think He already knows what is going on?"

"He might. But if He does, why wouldn't He have stepped in and given some guidance when we needed it?"

"Do you think He could have been testing us?"

"I don't know. I think I'm going to have a few questions besides the fate of the life on this planet."

"Me too, but remember who we are now. We don't want to give a bad impression."

"Bad impressions or not, we need some answers."

"First things first. We have to make contact."

"What do you suggest?"

"It's been so long since I existed in purely a spiritual sense, I don't remember. It seems that thought takes you where you want to be and that questions of reality and propriety were simple fact...there was no need for questions...everything existed in perfect order."

"Then if there were someone monitoring us, we would be part of their perfect order, wouldn't we?"

"You have a point, but I think I meant to say the existence in the spiritual realm was perfect. The idea for us would be to coincide with that order, thus achieving the perfect of all possible worlds. I want to say that the only imperfection of the spiritual world is that it is not physical. That's OK for Him and the spirits though, because to achieve the perfection they know in that world, sets them apart from us. They would like, however, the option of being a part of the physical world. That probably is why I'm so concerned about what is and isn't acceptable in their eyes. If we were ever able to bring this planet to perfection, we would automatically become part of the spiritual world...a playground for the spirits closest to God."

"I'll be damned! Do you really believe that?"

"I think if I were purely spiritual, with no tie to the physical world, I would long to experience the phenomena of the universe in a way that would allow a tangible sensual experience."

"I think I would too. I would long for your wind and rain. Yes definitely. I would miss the physical manifestations we have, even if we are imperfect."

"But you know, I think it would be well worth the effort to have this planet reach perfection in God's judgment. Can you imagine what it would be like to be in the physical and spiritual worlds at the same time?"

"That is slightly mind boggling isn't it?"

"There must be some way to verify all of this."

"When you think about it though, we have plenty of time. You're the expert, but even I can see this planet is far from perfect."

"Yes, but we must be constantly trying for perfection."

"You're all the time talking about one life form surviving at the expense of another. This is the physical world. The rules are different than those of the spiritual world. If we are going to strive for a perfection that other spirits can enjoy, then we must know the rules. What is acceptable and what is not."

"Every creature we saw today has one thing it's concerned about...survival, meaning overcoming those who prey on them and becoming that one superior creature at the top of the food chain. That is the creature who will have the intelligence to choose to end the chain. There will eventually be such a creature. Its evolution will be complete. When will we know this creature has arrived?

Surely this creature will consume other life forms. Will it be possible for this creature to be perfect in God's eyes?"

"That's a good question, and I don't have an answer. Somehow we must make contact with the Father. Let's both try. Meet me here tomorrow, same time and place."

"Goodbye. Oh! In case I didn't mention it, I still love you."

"I love you too. Goodbye."

Both spirits tried hard to make contact with the spiritual world from which they came. They both realized the separateness of the two worlds. The spiritual world was once again an existence beyond their comprehension. Yet there were certain aspects they could imagine and without realizing it for sure, they were quite accurate. The most important of these aspects were that the spirits dwelling in the fourth dimension were witnessing the phenomena of God's universe. The universe, in all its glory, held wonders to occupy the spirits, yet few and far between were heavenly bodies which had given birth to life forms, not to mention life forms of the complexity of those Yin and Yan were responsible for. Both were accurate in thinking that the Father would be interested in this world. They were also correct in their assumption that the spirits longed to be physically manifested. Witnessing the universe's natural processes were not the same as tangibly being a part of it.

"Did you have any luck?"

"No, did you?"

"No, I went to the outskirts of the atmosphere, but did not see anything."

"You know the more I try to remember, the more I imagine about being a spirit without the bonds of being part of a world."

"Me too. How do you remember it?"

"It seems that you have a central location, and you are aware of the universe, but you can't really be a part of it. Now I may be going a little far in saying this, but I think, if you really desire to be a part of the physical world you can request that it be done."

"Do you think that's how we ended up here?"

"The memory of it happening is gone, but I seem to remember being a spirit and wanting to be a part of the tangible world."

"I do too, but just like you, I don't remember the transition."

"I wonder how we both ended up on the same planet."

"It could have been a part of our request."

"Something about that bothers me though. Being able to be anywhere in the universe, in a spiritual sense, is a great freedom to give up since the alternative would be to be anchored in one place. Perhaps physical manifestation could be a punishment."

"For what? I thought we decided the spiritual world was perfect order."

"I did too, but there must still be room to go against the order, against God. I think that must be why you were always concerned about what would be acceptable to the Father."

"Do you think you would have ever gone against the Father?"

"I hope I never have. I think I'm probably one of those who requested tangible characteristics."

"Why?"

"I really don't think I would have enjoyed popping in and out of places just sight seeing the beautiful natural happening of the universe."

"Yes that would get boring."

"Do you think we could have known each other before we came to the planet?"

"I don't know. I suppose it's possible."

"Think we could have put in a joint request?"

"I don't know that either. Maybe we'll have a chance to find that out some day. I don't think it's important. We love each other now. That's all that really matters."

"You're right."

"I think what we've done with this planet probably ranks pretty high as far as spectacles go. Just look at this stuff."

"Do you think there would be room for more spirits on this planet?"

"Sure if they don't mind being animals."

"I could not see wanting to be something that knows only to survive by the methods these animals know. These animals don't have any choices. They still live by the rules of consume or be consumed. They're really not a direct creation of God. He made the universe, this planet, and us somewhere along the line. These creatures are a part of those natural wonders of our influence on the planet. They don't realize there is another world. No spirit would ever want to experience life the way these creatures do. Do you think the creature that will be ruler of the animal world will be perfect in the sense that it could be the bridge between the physical and spiritual worlds?"

"I'm not sure, but I think we should make it our goal to see that this creature does come to life. That could take a long time."

"If that's what it takes to bring the physical and spiritual worlds together, then it will be worth the trouble."

"Then we should get started."

"These huge animals that you are so proud of, I hate to say it, but they're just the same as small creatures as far as what motivates them. Even their size doesn't prevent them from falling prey to the smaller creatures that realize their vulnerability. Sooner or later they will be killed off."

"Why don't we rush things and kill them off ourselves?"

"They're among those at the top of the food chain. I don't know if we would be hurrying things or not."

"We're not masters of the planet for nothing. If we're ever going to influence the outcome of this evolutionary process to produce a creature that would lend itself for physical manifestation of spirits, then we must backtrack to the process to find an animal capable of great things. We must decide the criteria to use as a goal. When we find this creature then we submit it for approval."

"The way I see it we shouldn't intervene. It must evolve naturally. It must be the ruler of this world by its own merits. Otherwise it will not be able to survive among the other creatures. Anything less than this, if we do the selecting, then the creature will not develop the superior intellectual capacity we would desire to offer those of the spiritual world."

"Do you remember I told you all life would have us to contend with?"

"Yes."

"We've been dormant during the time these monsters evolved. Do you think they could survive the torment we have to offer?"

"You're intent on killing off these creatures."

"I don't think we should allow them to be obstacles to the creatures in contention for the position at the top of the chain."

"You're right, but let's not rush things. The creature must be able to survive just about anything we have to throw at him, won't he?"

"Yes. That criterion will allow us a forewarning of which one it will be."

"What other criteria will there be?"

"Of course we must think of the criteria God, our Father, would use in determining what he will and won't accept."

"What will that be though?"

"I would never try to second guess our Father, but I still feel that the creature would bring about the end to the food chain."

"I think you're right in that the creature must be at the top, but how will it end the chain? Something that evolves through the desire to be the ultimate creature, the one dominant over all the others, would always desire to demonstrate its supremacy. Won't it?" Won't it still kill for its food?"

"I don't know. Maybe since all the creatures are not spiritual beings, the food chain will always be. The problem may be of a nature we know nothing about."

"I suppose we'll have to cross that bridge when we get there then."

"Yeah, there's no sense trying to solve problems that haven't arrived yet."

"Are you thinking the same thing I am?"

"If you're thinking of sitting it out while the ultimate creature evolves, you've got another think coming. Not only do we have to throw everything we have at it, we need to witness what they go through. We have to know these creatures inside and out. Not to mention the fact that we just spent a period of who knows how long in dormancy. Sure it was relaxing, but I did miss life. It wasn't quite the same as before we lost our symmetry. The whole time I could think of nothing but you. Of course the knowledge that you were dormant, and would come after me at the appropriate time, allowed me not to fight time. I don't think I could be so restful again, especially not now."

"Well if we are going to keep up with this race for supremacy, I suggest we take time out first to celebrate this occasion. We've been without each other for years now, and we mastered the environment. Most of all, we've started well on its way, the chain of life we hope will someday close the gap between the physical and spiritual worlds."

"You're right. What would you like to do first?"

"Take a long look around and contemplate the world as it was and is now."

"We have come a long way, haven't we?"

"Yes but somehow I feel we have a long way to go yet."

"You're probably right, but let's not think of that now."

"Let's go."

"Tell me about life under the surface."

"Sure."

"You know everything on land had its beginnings in the sea."

"You mean to say everything started there?"

"Well yes. The algae were first so theoretically every life form can be traced to it. What I'm trying to say is that just about all the creatures on land are descendants of animals which tried to free themselves of the terror of the food chain below the surface. I don't know all the details, we were asleep, but yes, for the most part there are two almost separate food chains those above and below the surface."

"I wonder if our ultimate creature will command both worlds."

"Well, it won't do to have the most intelligent, not capable of being ruler of the entire planet."

"Ruler of everything, but us."

"Of course. Well Yin, we've come up with new criteria. Our champion will rule both worlds."

"The two worlds are so different. Are there many animals that live in both?"

"A few, but the majority won't outlive the obstacles we present. Of those who would survive, there are none who aren't already prey to another or that aren't simple plant eating species."

"Does that pose the same question to you as it does to me?"

"What's that?"

"Will our creature prey on others?"

"I'm sure if it does not kill for food, it would have to kill in self-defense. I would think if it killed in self defense, it would have the intelligence to know that the beast would be eaten if our creature didn't eat it itself. I really can't fathom how a creature would reach the top of the food chain without actually being a part of it. I don't see how a creature would find the end without being the end itself."

"I suppose we won't know the answers until they actually come up."

"I suppose not."

"What do you want to do now?"

The First Time

"Guess."

"You've got a one track mind!"

"No I don't. It's been eons since we've been together. What's wrong with a little fun?"

"I'm just teasing. Actually, I thought you'd never ask."

"Besides we've got a lot of work to do."

"Obstacles?"

"Yes. Some we don't even know of."

"Sounds like it could take a while."

"Then let's take our time with this reunion celebration."

"Good idea."

And the two did take a while. The commotion in itself sent many creatures into panic. When party time was over, it came time to put the creatures to the test. The first of which was something never before seen, not even by the spirits. Yan felt that the eons of no interference had produced a delicate stability in the planet. There were only a few volcanoes and they weren't very active. This caused the surface temperature to fall. In turn, the ice caps grew. One day the spirits were close to the caps, and Yin decided to make some rain for Yan. It was a spectacle for them both...snow. At first just seeing it was exciting, and then it started piling up. Yin was ecstatic. She rushed water spouts to fill clouds and dumped snow over the entire northern portion of the world. Things got a little out of hand, there were creatures trying to cope with freezing temperatures that were evolved during times of very active volcanoes. Needless to say, they didn't survive. Neither of the spirits was upset. This would be a part of life in the future, if there were animals not able to cope with it then they would be like so many other species who couldn't overcome the other obstacles the world presented them. This period lasted many years. Several life forms disappeared, but the survivors strove again to overcome the factors that must be contended with. Evolution never stopped. Of course the plant life changed its habits, and those creatures whose diet included or was plant life died. Yin and Yan were not regretful. They truly felt that elimination of those who would not survive was the charitable thing to do. The fact that it pushed the ultimate creatures into assuming its dominance was only a side benefit. There were many creatures which adapted to the cold. Those with the intelligence went south to the temperate climates. Those which couldn't adapt or escape the cold were no longer.

"We've eliminated a few. The ones that adapted will have to migrate when it's over, otherwise they will die too. Did you single out any creatures as showing promise?"

"There was one group that would eat plant life when it was on the move. They would hunt in packs probably because they were so small. They slept in trees to escape being the prey. There were a few other oddities about them, but I doubt they would ever be the top of the chain...they're not very aggressive."

"Sounds interesting, but it's still too soon to tell."

"Could there be a possibility of the creature coming from below the surface?"

"No I don't think so. The period of those creatures trying to escape the chain by leaving the sea, is over. Size is a defense...the larger the creature, the fewer the others have to prey on it. Another is safety in numbers. The ones at the top of the chain down there will never know life on land. I can imagine an intelligent land animal taking advantage of the sea's population, but never the other way around."

"We must be getting closer. We've ruled out the creatures of the sea. There aren't many land creatures left."

"What about flying creatures? You know more about them."

"Their evolution has all but stopped. I don't think they're interested in being dominant, as long as they have food; the freedom of flight is all they're concerned about. There are a few species that don't even care for flight. They are easy prey...again safety in numbers keeps them alive."

"Then we can focus on the species of land animals in the temperate zone."

"Something I was thinking--of the few species we haven't ruled out there are two types, animals on all four limbs and those which stand on their hind limbs. Do you think it is a safe assumption that those who use their front limbs for other purposes than transporting themselves have an advantage over the rest?"

"Yes, they probably do. But they must still prove themselves to be at the top of the chain by proving their dominance."

"I'm not positive, but I think I've figured out which one it will be."

"Don't drag it out! Which one?"

"The one I was talking about earlier."

"They're too small to ever be at the top."

"I haven't observed them much, but I think they rely on mental capabilities more than their physical attributes."

"Where are some of these creatures?"

"They move in packs like I said. I haven't seen any lately. If they are the ones though, it's going to be a long time before we can show them to the Father."

"If they are the top of the chain though, their evolution must be close to being complete."

"Perhaps, we'll have to wait and see."

The spirits observed the creatures for a while, and then retreated with Yin in the lead.

"Why did you come here Yan?"

"Because this is the place I last enjoyed some semblance of peace."

"If you have something to say, say it now!"

"Those scrawny little creatures will never amount to anything. What spirit would ever give up the freedom of roaming the entire universe to experience the life of one of those?"

"So you want to give up again?"

"I'm simply frustrated by the whole thing. I would like some time to myself to contemplate my situation."

"Take all the time you want but don't interfere. You've already given your word on that."

"Please! Leave me alone!"

"OK. I love you. Things will be alright."

"Goodbye."

And the two parted. Yin in her favorite spot between the moon and the planet and Yan, so upset he could never find solace, roamed the planet contemplating the past.

Yin noticed the difference in the gentle pull. All of a sudden, she was in the height of her bubble. She did not pull away though; she knew there was a reason.

"Don't be afraid. I come on a mission of peace."

The First Time

"Who are you?"

"I am a spirit. I have been watching you from a distance for many years."

"Are you the spirit of the moon?"

"No. There is no spirit embodied in the moon, although I consider it a second home. A long time ago, I located myself here and noticed the life on the planet. I kept it my secret until recently."

"Then you've been spying on us?"

"Yes, in a manner of speaking. But relax; I am on your side. I could be of great importance to you, if you let me."

"Why are you talking to me instead of both Yan and me?"

"First of all there's a problem of logistics. You are much closer to me than Yan; also you seem very upset by the turn of events. I wanted to comfort you with news of great importance."

"What is that?"

"I would like to tell you and Yan, at the same time."

"But you do say there's no need for me to be upset?"

"Yes, in fact, I think what I have to say will cheer you up quite a bit."

"Let's hurry! Where would be a good place to meet?"

"I've really never been located on your planet. Would it be an intrusion for me to do that now?"

"No, you're welcome. Wait for us on that island, I'll go find Yan."

"This will be an adventure for me."

"Enjoy yourself. I'll be back as soon as I can find him."

"OK."

Finding Yan was somewhat of a problem. The last encounter the pair had put him in a state of depression. Their dreams were not coming to light. He began to wonder if he was being punished. It took Yin days to find him. He was watching a group of the creatures they had determined would be the end of the chain. They were not a promising group.

"Yan!"

"Yes. Yin, is that you?"

"Of course it's me. Who else could it be? I've been looking everywhere for you. Come on. We have a visitor!"

"What do you mean a visitor?"

"It's a spirit who's been watching us."

"It's a spirit's prerogative to locate where it wants, and this one has been located on the moon and watching us. Come on, it says it has some good news."

"I don't like the idea of being watched."

"It never interrupted."

"Two's company, three's a crowd."

"You're being difficult."

"This is our planet."

"It's God's planet, and I think this spirit has been in contact with the Father."

The First Time

"I think we're still not ready for the Father."

"At least listen to him."

"OK, but this spirit interferes, and he's asking for trouble."

"I've never seen you like this."

"I'm sorry, it's just the situation. I won't give him any trouble."

"Then come on. It supposedly has some good news."

"You lead the way."

The trip was not a short one, but Yin's excitement, hurried things along.

"We're all here, what do you have to tell us?"

"First, I'd like to say it's a pleasure to finally meet you Yan. You are a spirit of good judgment."

"Hey buddy, save the flattery. What's the idea of invading our privacy?"

"It was purely accidental. I never have and never will interrupt in matters that are of a personal nature to you and Yin. Knowing that you two cannot go to the Father yourselves, I took it upon myself to make your progress known to Him. I hope I haven't overstepped the boundaries of propriety."

"No, you haven't!" Yin injected, to avoid letting Yan remark. "We were at one point trying to find an audience with the Father, but couldn't get in touch. I know, speaking for myself, that I am glad you've made Him aware of our situation, but do you know our motivations?"

"Not personally, but the Father says He can guess what you have in mind. He told me to make myself available as a mediator, of course only if that would meet with your approval."

"That's fine with me! What about you Yan?"

"I suppose we could use some help at this point."

"Would you give us a full account of your meeting with the Father?"

"Certainly. I recalled some of the events after the two of you first met. The Father knew of your physical manifestation, but decided not to interrupt. Apparently, He was not too happy with the idea...something to do with temptations. He was not surprised to hear of simple life forms, but did not understand why you chose to let them evolve as you did. He realizes you must have some reasons, but only the Eternal Father knows that, and He has indicated a desire to reserve judgment. He does encourage communications on these matters though. By the way, He sends his blessings on your relationship...He is proud to have seen you get along so well. It has been my own observation that compliments of this nature seldom go unrewarded."

"Did you hear that Yan! We're on good terms. They want us!"

"It does give the day a turn for the better doesn't it!"

"As usual, Yin is bursting with exuberance," said the mediator.

"What's to get so excited about? We're by no means a success yet. There's much to be done. I think first we should show you the planet and explain what we have in mind."

"That would be nice. I've been wondering for a long time, what was going on down here."

Having accepted on good faith, the spirit's trust, Yan began with the preliminaries. "You must understand some things first. Yin and I don't remember anything of the spiritual world. One day after an unknown length of time we discovered each other. We both have a conception of life as a spirit, but we really don't remember.

[65]

"Stop right there. Before the end of the audience I had with the Father, He gave me some information about you. I did not mention it yet, because I thought it would break the trust I'm trying to build."

"Please! Tell us what He said!" Yin said, sensing the answers to many questions.

"I hope it doesn't discourage you."

"If you're looking for trust, be quick and report what you found out." Yan was getting impatient.

"The Father told me you are of the same world that all spirits inhabit. Long ago the two of you grew bored of simply witnessing the marvels of the universe. One day the two of you were discussing the dilemma and decided to seek an audience with the Father. Your request was granted and you met with Him. He tried to warn you of the problems that would arise, but you insisted on requesting physical manifestation. This was new to the spiritual world, and when everyone else heard of it, it seemed as though you would start a fad. The Father told you each to go and choose the place you wished to be and return to Him. Both of you, without conferring with the other, came to this familiar place. This was a favorite rendezvous for both of you to discuss your fates. You should have discussed the locations of where you would be physically manifested, but you didn't. You both returned with the same location individually requesting the Father to grant your wishes. He did so and told the general audience, many of whom were choosing their sites. Many spirits came to see the beautiful lives you were living together. They were sadly disappointed. Not only were you inactive individually, but you did not even sense the presence of one another. You were two of the closest spirits in the spiritual world, and you were facing an eternity of loneliness. Needless to say, there were no more physical manifestations."

The mediator continues, 'We had all forgotten, resolved not to become tangible entities. It was so long that you yourselves forgot the life in the spiritual realm. As for myself, I never really knew of your plight. When it happened I told myself that type of life was not for me, and didn't think of you again. After so long, the other spirits gave up on you too. It was the closest thing to death any of us had ever witnessed in our world. They stopped visiting this grave...at that time it was the only depressing issue. They didn't want to face it so they let the memory fade. There is much for me to tell you about the spiritual world, but that can wait. I kept your revival between me and the Father. He was very happy to hear you were active. He would like to come and visit you. He remembers you as a team among the most cherished of spirits. He wants me to return as soon as possible with all the news I can."

"Yan, we can't disappoint the Father. Let's tell Him about our plans."

"Didn't you just hear him? There's no more physical manifestation of spirits. Those plans are defunct."

"Spirits chose not to because of what happened to us. They don't know what it can mean."

"Even at that, we are failing to produce a creature a spirit would want to be."

"We're not finished yet."

"Listen you two; the Father seemed anxious to hear from you. Isn't there something I can tell Him that is not controversial to you?"

Yin volunteered. "Simply give Him our love. Tell Him, as usual, He was right about the dangers of being physical. Tell Him we're sorry for disappointing Him, but we're trying to make up for it. We can explain why we've allowed the life to evolve, but of course He knows why. Incidentally, we're very proud of it. We think it goes unmatched in the universe. I hope I'm not being presumptuous in saying that."

"You really aren't."

"That's great. I suppose the last thing is to tell Him the sooner we get together, the better. Yan, do you have anything to add?"

"I just want to say that I've missed Him."

"OK, that does it. Oh! I almost forgot there is news from the spiritual world you should know about. It happened not too long after you two left."

"My goodness, if it's still important after such a long length of time we must have really missed something big."

"It is big, but be glad you missed it. There's been a schism. I can't go into details, but there are two worlds now. Our world, that still recognizes the Father as supreme and keeps our spirit pure, is called heaven. Those who no longer are of pure spirit follow Satan. He was a powerful spirit who chose to transgress the Fathers' wishes. He corrupted many spirits and they were all cast out into a world we refer to as hell. The two worlds are exact opposites. There is no co-existence. You are either of heaven or hell, there is no middle ground. The Father told me to assure you that you are still a part of His world and knows you would never choose the world of sin."

Yan recalled, "I remember thinking there was the possibility to go against the perfect order of the Father's way. I just didn't think there would ever be someone to want something different. Tell the Father we love His world too much to even contemplate crossing over."

"I will. Is there anything else?"

"As Yin said, we look forward to having Him here."

"I'll be back as soon as possible."

The spirit left the two alone. Emotions were high and communications were silent. Neither could put to words the hundreds of issues running through their minds. A sudden unexpected bolt of lightning reminded them how to communicate.

"Hey Yan, you're excited aren't you?"

"Yeah, it's been a tough day. I've been the lowest and highest I've ever been. Are you feeling alright?"

"I feel great! That lightning didn't hurt anything either."

"Sorry. I didn't even feel it coming."

"Now I believe you're easy."

"I love you."

"I love you too."

"Listen, he could be back here any minute. Let's get ready."

"There's nothing to do, except wait."

"Come on. We have to do something special. The Father Himself is coming."

"Relax. Tell me what we could do and we'll do it"

Yin tried to think of something, but couldn't. "We should at least think of what to say."

"I remember now. I never tried to plan an audience with the Father because He always knew everything. Planning the conversation just led to confusion and disappointment."

"We could at least plan a show of our mastery of the planet."

"He's the Father. He already knows,"

Dumbfounded, an awkward period of silence passed.

"Then what do we do?"

"Wait. Shoot the breeze, anything to pass the time."

The First Time

"Anything?"

"Yan! God the Father Almighty is coming and you have the unmitigated gall to think about making love."

"You're right. You know He warned me about the temptations of physical existence."

"He warned me too."

"I don't think they're all that bad."

"You're going to end up in hell."

"You just heard the spirit say that the Father knew we would never cross into that world."

"There's a first time for everything, and this may be the first time the Father is wrong."

"Yin, relax. This conversation is getting out of hand."

"Better the conversation be unleashed than you."

"I think we should just wait on the Father."

"Fine, I'll be in my usual place."

"Yin we should meet Him together."

"Not if you can't be civil."

"I love you."

"Don't change the subject."

"Do you love me?"

"At the moment, that would require some thought."

"If you do love me, don't embarrass me by running off by yourself when we're expecting the Father any minute."

"OK. I won't run off, but promise no funny business until He leaves."

"I was just teasing you when I said that."

"Oh yeah. Where's that lightning coming from?"

"I don't know. Besides that would at least be half your fault."

"I didn't do anything."

"Nothing, except being that pure spirit I talked to thousands of times, wanting you to be embodied somewhere so I could touch you."

"You didn't say that when you talked me into physical manifestation."

"If I'd said that, you would've never done it."

"Did you know we were coming to the same planet?"

"No."

"You loved me before we did it."

"Yes."

"You thought I'd rather be physical, than spiritual."

"Yes, after a bit of convincing conversation."

"You were right."

"Then wait on the Father with me."

"Of course I love you."

The First Time

"I love you too."

An ominous voice interrupted. "There's nothing more amusingly gratifying than a couple of love birds in their mating dance."

In a harmonizing tone of shock, the two let out "Oh, Father!"

"My timing is perfect as usual. Wouldn't you say?"

Yan took the lead. "Yes, just like everything else you have a hand in."

"We don't really understand. How did it happen?"

"Yan we've talked about temptation, how I left room for decision. It was one of my beloved confidants who gave in to it."

"Satan?"

"Yes."

"I'm surprised. He was quite a noble spirit."

"It was that sense of nobility that led him astray. Many trusted him. Many followed him into darkness. His promises were alluring. Most of his followers are trying to find their way back to the light."

"Will you take them back?"

"It's like someone said, once you've lost perfection you can never gain it back. Even if it is recovered, it is not true perfection; it is marred by the memory of imperfection."

"Speaking for myself, I can identify with that. We took this planet that was perfectly symmetrical, now look at it. Our aspirations lay with the hopes of bringing it back to perfection. Please tell us now. Are we holding on in an impossible mission?"

"I have much to say concerning the two of you and this planet. I love you both very dearly. I have missed you. Many were the times I felt inclined to come and counsel with you. My confidence in you kept me away."

"In the talks we had before I made you this planet, I warned you of the troubles I thought you were sure to encounter. It is obvious you forgot the talks, but you have done well."

"You'll never know how happy I was that both of you chose the same location. For the sake of the spiritual world, I was pleased that you didn't discover each other in the beginning. If you had, there would have been many more to follow your example. It would have been very lonely if all my spirits joined the physical realm."

"I suppose you don't recall saying that perfection in the physical realm would be a rare thing. Your planet here is not an exception. Even before you came here, it was not perfect. It lacked cognizant life. You were the element that brought it life, but as usual, even when you're dealing with perfect beings, two mouths and one apple will always find fault, no matter how the apple is sliced. I had confidence in you though, and as usual, I was right. You had your problems with each other, but I gave you both talents for coping and you've made great progress. No, the planet was not perfect, is not and may never be."

"You have brought to life a dream, but I'm sorry to disappoint you. I find it a dangerous idea to take the perfection of a loyal spirit and allow it to physically experience the life of an animal the epitome of a long time of evolution catering to survival in a world of sin. Even if these animals do decide to end this chain of death it would still be a great risk. The temptation would be there with great strength. Only an equal strength in resolve to escape the temptation would stop the chain. I would not risk the physical manifestation of any of my spirits in these beings."

"Father, we have labored over this for many years now. We have sight of the being we feel will be the end of the chain. All life on this planet has, since its beginning, strove for survival, only to produce the being that would be the end. Please don't say that all has been in vain. There has been too much sacrificed for the sake of this being."

"You know me better than that. I'm sure you have had much heart ache connected with your decision to allow this chain to go on. You have done well. There has never been a marriage of the spiritual and physical other than you. These life forms have never had spirit. They felt the pain, learned, sacrificed for what they hoped would be a world different from the world they knew. They had a blind faith that a reward would be theirs someday. They do deserve reward."

"I could use more spirits...strong spirits like those at the end of the chain. I can't allow those spirits of mine now to know the cumulative knowledge these beings would have. How I propose to solve these two problems is to give your ultimate creature the potential for an everlasting spirit that would serve only Me. You realize this gives you a great deal of work. You must allow this creature to evolve, not interrupting the natural selection process. Then contact me and I will give it meaning...a spirit with the potential for life everlasting with Me."

"You mean to tell us that we'll be responsible for bringing forth creatures that will have spirit like us?"

"No, not like you. They will have the burden of overcoming the temptations associated with their origin. I also believe the forces aligned with Satan, will try to pull them into his world. It will not be easy for these beings. I ask you now to stand behind them; after all, they would not be here if it weren't for you."

"You have given us a great honor. We will do our best not to disappoint you."

"Send for me when the evolution has stopped."

"Thank you for coming."

He was gone and the two could not speak for the intense feelings of happiness and self-actualization. After so long it became a feeling that would not be silent.

"Can you believe it?" Yan said.

"It's hard, but we have to. This is much better than what we had planned."

"I would have never dreamed it would come to this. We actually have the chance to give life to spirits."

"I'm sure this will be better than trying to give spirits to life."

"I have a feeling though that there are many obstacles to overcome."

"It seems to me the evolution has all but run its course with the creatures we have sighted as the end of the chain."

"The Father spoke as if it would be a while before it was complete."

"He must know something we don't."

"He knows a lot we don't."

"I suppose we'll have to continue being patient then."

"Yes, and for some reason I think the completion of the evolution will only be the beginning."

"I feel as though I have new life."

"Me too. He set my mind at ease about many things. I love you more than ever. Look what we have done."

"I love you too. I feel like nothing can stop us."

"We must take care not to fall into Satan's world."

"I am still shocked that it was him to transgress against the Father. I remember him quite well now...very strong-willed, proper, with an attitude of superiority that alienated him from everyone else. There could never be a bond between him and the other spirits. I mean a bond of love."

"Let's worry about that when the time comes."

"I think it's probably all part of the same burden for the beings to overcome."

"Probably, but let's do first things first."

"Let's go check on the creatures."

"I know they don't have a spirit yet, but let's call them beings as if they did."

"Good Idea. Do you know where they are right now?"

"I think so, follow me."

The two spirits found some of the beings and began their observation.

"Yan, I've seen more graceful creatures."

"It doesn't matter how graceful they are. There's plenty of time for them to develop gracefulness."

"What should we be watching for?"

"How they differ from the other creatures."

"They seem to have a close sense of inner dependence."

"That's probably one of the factors that allowed them to come so far. With their size, I'm sure they'd be easy prey for many other creatures unless they defended themselves as a group."

"It doesn't appear to be safety in numbers though."

"No. You're right. It appears they use strategy. See how some of them watch for predators, while the others go about their business."

"There are very few other animals that do that."

"Another thing I like about them is that their diet isn't purely the predators they killed. They eat many types of plant life as well."

"I have my doubts that they'll ever stop killing though. They come from a long line of those who killed for survival."

"Remember, the Father said more of the creatures have a spirit."

"Even at that though, shouldn't the end of the line mean no more bloodshed?"

"I don't understand what the Father had to say about that. I don't think we should be too concerned if these creatures continue to kill for self-defense or to demonstrate their dominance. I won't be upset if they kill because of their inherent need."

"I know other creatures will never have spirit, but don't you think the day will come when they stop killing for any purpose?"

"I can't see how all animal life would escape the realities of the chain, and there will always be that creature that no other creature can prey upon."

"I think we may be trying to second guess the Father."

"You're right; we must concentrate on doing what He asked us to do. I believe I'm right in not being concerned with the creatures eating habits. We should see to it that the creature develops physically and mentally though."

"How will we know when it's time to present it to the Father?"

The First Time

"I'm not sure, but there's still plenty of time for that."

"What should we do now?"

"We will eventually test it to see if it can survive all the obstacles we have to throw at them."

"You want to do that now?"

"No, but before we can present it as the ultimate creature, it should know how to deal with our natural obstacles."

"It seems to me we're going to have a long wait."

"It won't take as long as some of the things we've been through."

"This marriage of physical and spiritual has me excited."

"If we do as we're told, it will come about faster."

"It will still be a long time."

"We don't have to keep a vigil over these beings."

"Are you thinking the same thing I am?"

"Yes, but I remember the warning the Father gave me about being a physical entity."

"I remember too, but there's no escaping it now."

"Let's get away from the beings."

"Yan! You're not ashamed for us to share this, are you?"

"To be honest, after what the Father said about temptation, I'm concerned about the example we may be setting."

"They don't know us as beings. It would just be a natural phenomenon of the planet to them."

"You're right, but wouldn't it disturb the creatures?"

"They have to get used to it sooner or later."

"OK. You know we deserve to celebrate some. For the first time since that first whirlpool, we have something to celebrate. Let's take it easy. We don't want to hurt the beings."

The couple produced several days of the most severe weather the beings had ever witnessed, but when it was over, the couple had satisfied their urge for physical gratification, and the beings had learned a thing or two."

"They came through it with no problem. Did you see them under those covers?"

"Yes, they're animal skins. I never noticed them before. I wonder how they got them."

"Obviously they took them from the animals they preyed upon. Yan these creatures are much more intelligent than we've given them credit for. We must watch them more closely."

"You know they couldn't have taken those skins without some type of implement to help them."

"Look! Can you see that female crashing something with a rock?"

"Yes! She's preparing something to eat!"

"But she's using a rock!"

"I know! It's incredible! There's no other animal with the intelligence to do that. How could we not know about this?"

"It's easy. We've never spent much time with these creatures. Beings, I mean beings."

"They are above the creature stage aren't they?"

"They definitely are. The Father must have known this though. I don't know what else to expect of these beings."

"There must be more evolution to come. He said we must see to it that their evolution is complete."

"I'm astonished with them now. What else could there be?"

"I don't know, but we're going to find out."

"Let's keep a vigil over them to try and be more knowledgeable about them."

"Look at their stance. It looks like they want to stand straight up, but can't."

"OK, that's one thing that should happen...they'll stand. What else should happen?"

"Well I'm sure they communicate much better than other animals, but they just use signs and groans. I'm sure they will develop a more intricate system of communication."

"OK, that's another. What else?"

"I don't know. You look and see."

"Have you noticed there seems to be a chain of command? The older and bigger males aren't doing anything. It seems as though they dominate everything going on. Do you know what that means in and of itself?"

"I'm afraid to verbalize it."

"Then I will. I always thought that to find the creature at the top of the chain would be the end to dominance. I never imagined that the creatures would set up their own system of hierarchy to allow a continuance of the chain, thus allowing a perpetuation of the same struggle to be the beings at the top of the chain."

"This is terrible."

"I know, but what can we do? We must see to it that evolution does come to an end. But I was thinking about that. Will there ever be an end to evolution? Even if all goes as planned, will the being ever find a way to not be confronted with situations that would cause obstacles and thus more evolution?"

"That's a good question that I don't have an answer to. Remember the Father said to send for Him when evolution stopped. We will be satisfied when the being stands erect and develops a way to communicate in a more sophisticated manner. These things will naturally occur. I can't see any other advancement after this happens. All I see we need to do is to wait for this to occur and see to it the beings know how to deal with the weather. If it handles the rest of our obstacles as easily as it did rain, then it will have no problems. It seems we're in a waiting game again."

"First we should observe the beings just to get an idea of their capabilities."

"That shouldn't take long."

"No, but I am curious about them."

"Oh, don't get me wrong, I am too. I'm just very disappointed the end is not the end."

"I am too... Let's watch them."

The couple observed the beings for a long time. They had mixed emotions as to whether or not the beings would be acceptable for the Father's wishes, but there was the overriding factor that the Father knew they would be the ones. Over the years the observation period lasted, the couple exposed the beings to every weather related obstacle. The beings had no problems dealing with them. The evolution progressed. The beings eventually stood erect. Their system of communication also progressed...hand signals were used less and less; the grunts and groans became more and more intricate. There came no doubt their dominance over the animal world was complete. From a few encounters in nature, fire was mastered and used in various ways to fight the cold, ward off would be predators, and to cook food. These developments were long in coming for the couple. They never interfered, allowing the evolution to take its natural course. They realized the beings had passed the points they promised would be considered the completion of evolution, but they also realized it was not the end. There would never be an end. It was time to present to the Father for whatever were his purposes, these creatures. It was time for them to take on the new role as the only life with a spirit.

"Have you had any contact with the spirit who observes from the moon?"

"Not recently. I've sensed him watching every once and awhile. If he's not there now, it won't be too long before he's back. I'll see if he's there now."

Yin went to the place between the planet and the moon to see if the mediator was there.

"Hello. Are you there?"

"Yes, I've been expecting you. You two must be ready to have the Father return."

"Well there have been some developments that cause some problems."

"What's that?"

"The Father said to send after Him when the evolution was complete. We've realized that it will never be complete. As soon as the Father left, we set some standards that would signal the completion and the beings or creatures have met those standards. We're not sure what to do, but we think it would be best to consult with the Father."

"I know He is very interested in success here. I will contact Him and relay your problems. I feel sure He will want to see you. Prepare for His coming."

"Thank you."

"Thank you for allowing me the privilege of being a part of this. I will be back directly."

Again the pair was at a loss as to how to prepare for the Father. It did not matter much...as soon as He was contacted by the mediator He came to the planet.

"My long lost loved ones, you have brought the creatures to their potential."

Yan did the talking for the two of them. "No Father. We don't see the end to their potential. They have met certain standards we said would signal the completion of their evolution, but they have imposed a system which perpetuates the conflict which is the root of evolution. We thought you would want to know about this."

"I feel as though the choice to perpetuate the struggle these creatures are the end result of, is the work of Satan. Otherwise, these creatures would be enjoying a life of contentment, peace, and harmony among themselves and the world they have championed. I felt this might happen...Satan is too smart to allow something as beautiful as that to exist without a struggle. I feel that, unfortunately, there will be a very long struggle for these beings to overcome the influence Satan is sure to invoke upon them."

"There is one chance for these creatures to escape his clutches. I will choose one man I feel will have the insight and courage not to give into Satan's world. Also there will be one woman to accompany him. I will isolate them in a place where they can flourish. They will be masters of this place, having the cumulative knowledge of the evolution which raised them above all other life. From them I will take the fear which perpetuates evolution. To them I will give the same spirit I gave you. This spirit is a part of Me. All the other creatures who accept life from Satan on this planet will be destroyed, thus leaving the fate of all who died before them in the hands of My chosen. It will be up to them whether or not life for them and their descendants will be a beautiful one with Me or a continuation of struggle with Satan. From now on these creatures are beings with the choice of life or death."

The two spirits were shocked. They never realized the Father would wipe out life of any description, but they did realize they were just like Him, and if it meant the only hope for more spirits to populate His kingdom, then they too would have made the same decision. This realization also begged the question. "Would this be the last time the Father would have to show His wrath?"

The Father did not delay. There was a short search among one clan of the creatures to find the chosen male. He was neither young nor old and seemingly typical of all the men of the groups. The Father did sense a desire in the man for a female a little younger than he. Somehow, the two simply met and walked away from the group. This usually would not have been tolerated, but not a word was said.

When the two were out of sight from the group, they lay down beside each other and went into a blissful sleep. All the other creatures, which were caught in Satan's power and realizing they were condemned to die, naturally hastened the inevitable. The Father did not need to enter into the matter. The two awoke after the horror was over, and realized they were the dominant of all on the planet. The burden of struggle for the top was over, and they realized their decisions no longer were made in the light of what would get them closer to the top. Now the choice took on connotations of what should be, not what would be. The two began to walk, noticing no differences in their world except the freedom from struggle which made their planet a paradise.

"Yan and Yin, you have done well. I am glad now that you exercised your right to become part of the physical world even if I sorely missed your example in your former world. I ask you now to continue your lives here as sentinels. Satan is still loose and nothing would please him more than to ruin our efforts here. It will be many years before his influence is overcome. Don't be disappointed when this world is again subjected to his pain. I wish you a long period of bliss with your beautiful creation. Enjoy while you can. Send for Me when it comes to an end. Goodbye."

"Yin, this is the "someday" we've been waiting for."

"I'm sorry, but I'd like to reserve the day when we are free of Satan's influence for good as my "someday.""

"Still, we should take pride and pleasure in this. We have seen through all the pain and reached the point when the life we chose not to end resulted in a marriage of the spiritual and physical worlds. We should be jubilant, but you hold back. I need you to be happy, but you refuse."

"I'm sorry Yan. I am happy but the happiness is tainted by the knowledge that at any time it could come to an end. You're right though. The marriage of spirit and life is something I've always wanted to see. Let's look over our planet to see what we have done...a honeymoon for us and our children."

"Where do you want to go first?"

"Do you remember that island where we spent so many years waiting for that green stuff to take over the planet?"

"Yes. I've never let that volcano die."

"You must have read my mind."

"I knew someday we would look back on that decision and be glad that we did what we did."

"Well I'm glad you didn't say I told you so, but you did tell me so and I love you for it."

The First Time

"Keep that up and we're going to scare the other honeymooners with an electrical storm. Let's go!"

"I'm right behind you."

Yan took the long way there at a very slow pace in order to see all the different life forms they could. They had never taken the time to stop and look at various creatures that pulled themselves out of the depths of the green sea. Realizing they were responsible for so much life made them quiver with pride. The thought that the food chain had made it possible for a creature to be part of the spiritual world allowed them to watch the chain in action and not regret its conception. The couple arrived at the island which had not changed much since they left.

"It's been a long time since we left this place hasn't it?"

"I'll never forget the time you made your first tidal wave here."

"How about trying to see if I can do it again?"

"Let me get the fires up first."

"OK, you ready?"

"Yes."

"Here it comes!"

Yan met the wall of water with an explosion of fire. The two skipped all the preliminaries and proved they still had what it took to make a spectacle in nature.

"OK buddy! You proved your point. How would some nice gentle rain feel after that?"

"Don't think I'm getting feeble in my old age, but that sounds very nice."

"How would you like a long lingering round of heat lightning?"

"That sounds good. How long do you think we can keep it up?"

"Well I could last a few weeks, but we need to get back and check on the newlyweds."

"I almost forgot. What do you think they're doing?"

"How many guesses do I get?"

"Just one."

"I have a feeling that's all I need."

"Do you really want to look in on them?"

"We do have to make sure they aren't giving into satanic influences."

"How could Satan mess up making love?"

"I'm not putting anything past him."

"Do we need to go now?"

"In a little while, you know we deserve some time to ourselves."

"I think the devil's got a hold on you."

"The only thing that's got a hold on me is you."

"This is getting out of hand. Let's go check on our pride and joy."

"I want to ask you something first."

"Go ahead."

"Would you promise to stick with me here until Satan is overcome? It seems as though this world has become of great importance to the

Father. We know Satan's influence will come to light here someday. We also know he will be overcome. Would you stay here with me until all this comes to pass?"

"You and I have been through so much. How do you think I could give up all you and I have sacrificed for? I will stay here with you to see the day that all our dreams come to fruition."

"I love you more each day. Let's check on our legacy."

"I'm beside you."

The two left their hideaway and again inspected the best of all possible worlds. On their arrival, they were shocked to see it did not take long for the pair to fall from the paradise they had been bestowed.

"Yin. Do you think we could have helped avoid this if we had stayed with them?"

"No the Father gave them their own spirit and judgment. We would not be able to influence them. The decision is theirs."

"Do you think there were satanic influences?"

"As I understand it, Satan causes one to consider the alternative to a decision made with good faith. It's easy to see the correct decision and usually no time is devoted to any alternatives. I thought these two were virgin to all factors. Apparently this knowledge of evolution has caused them to consider the side of decision which propagates the continuance of life in the darkness we hoped they'd escape. I hate to say it, but I think we should tell the Father."

"If you'll find the mediator, I'll watch these two."

"I'll be back soon."

Yin found the mediator quickly...he was anxious to see how things went. Hesitantly, he went for the Father. All four of them met to discuss the problems. The Father addressed the three.

"I'd hoped it would have been longer, but I also knew that taking these two from a world of sin and expecting them to forget their ways was hoping for too much. It would have been nice. Yan you remember about perfection, I wonder if it was the memory of imperfection that caused them to turn aside the perfection they were offered. It really doesn't matter now. These two must again populate the world. To aid this, I will make the woman more fertile. Of course I am not giving up hope. We will try again to bring these spiritual beings into a peace that will last forever. If you two are ever freed from this you've started, and it works out that I can use these beings where before I had only spirits. I promise you will be rewarded. Will you stay with it?"

Yin answered. "It is our life now. We will stay."

"Don't give up hope. Goodbye."

The Father was gone. The mediator said his farewells. "Good luck with the efforts to repopulate. I won't be keeping a constant vigil...the fight against Satan requires full strength in our world. The Father knows all. If He says there will be a time, it will be. Remember to love each other...you have a long way to go. I'll check with you periodically. Good luck! I'll see you later."

The two were alone again. Their feeling was familiar. At least this time they were only waiting for a few generations of the premier couple to come forth.

"Yan. If all we have to do is to wait for them to populate the world again, can't we sneak off and enjoy ourselves for a while?"

"We should wait and see to it they get a good start."

"Will the children have a spirit like their parents have?"

"Yes and never facing the dominance of others should allow a change in the way they think, at least for the first few generations."

"Then the offspring would actually be closer to paradise than their parents?"

"Yes but they will be taught by their parents who still have the memory of the chain instilled in them."

"How will we ever get them past the memories and influence of their ancestors?"

"I'm afraid we'll have to leave that up to the Father."

At this point, one of those prolonged silences interrupted. That old familiar sense hit both the spirits. The knowledge that they waited a long period to pass allowed them the silence without a breach of the bond that kept them so close. Without realizing, the silence lasted several months.

"Yan are you there?"

"Yes, what's the matter?"

"The woman is pregnant! Look."

"You're right. She's so big she could be having triplets!"

"She's not that big, but she's due any minute."

"You think you'd like to do that?"

"Wait until you see her deliver, you'll gain a new perspective that will give that question more meaning. Have you ever thought about being physically manifested as one of the beings?"

"Yeah, it crossed my mind."

"And?"

"I think I'd like it. It would certainly be a change, and I might be able to further the cause."

"I don't think I'd like it."

"Not if we did it together?"

"How could that happen?"

"We would need help from the Father of course, but we could occupy the body of two beings born about the same time. The chances of finding each other would be good. The only problem would be that just as we were manifested as a planet and forgot the spirit life, we would again forget who we were if we were manifested as a being. So there we'd be, roaming around looking for each other, not really knowing why, and not able to recognize each other when we did meet."

"How could you further the cause if you didn't know who you were?"

"I'm sure my spirit wouldn't change. I'd still approach decisions the same way."

"I'll bet the body of a beautiful girl would influence you."

"What girl could ever hit me like a tidal wave?"

"If I were the girl, I could."

"I bet."

The two spirits continued to watch the couple. The first baby came, then another, and another. All this time the family enjoyed being away from the example of those who survived the killing, those who were the victors in the battle of domination. This group also survived to take their place in the battle between good and evil. They sided with Satan, and he made it his business to see to it, that those who received the breath of life from the Father would not escape the temptations of the world they should have left behind. There was nothing Yin and Yan could do about it. Many years passed, the descendants of the premier couple lost sight of the world without conflict. The time came when they were all back to the hopeless situation of dominate or be dominated. Yan and Yin did not give up hope though. Again they sent for the Father when their mediator showed up to check the situation.

"We don't know what we're going to say when He does come, but we don't know what else to do."

"You see no way to influence these creatures?" interjected the mediator.

"Perhaps if we were once again free spirits we could guide them through the right paths, but we are the physical world...we no longer have the freedom to be a part of your world. Could you convince some strong spirits to come and exercise the powers they have on spiritual beings?"

"There are problems with that. There is the matter of priority...all the spirits left with the Father, consider it more important to protect the sanctity of our world. The Father does want this planet to bring forth His fruits though. I'll tell Him you need His help.

When He heard the cry for help from His favorite couple, He was there.

"I had hoped it would be easy to sever the ties of the evil which brought these creatures forth. It seems that all I do lately is try to conquer the works of Satan. More and more I see him reaching into My world and spoiling the beauty of My creations. Are there any descendants of the two I gave this world to who hold to My ways, or has Satan ruined all of our work?"

"There are some, one tribe, that has passed down a way of life which does coincide with your laws. The leader of this tribe is very old and his family will succumb to the evil with each new member that comes from the world outside them. Other than this man, there is no one left with the spirit to guide any creatures to your world."

"Then it seems obvious to Me. Why haven't you done this before? You must never again take the chance of loosing the spirit as you have."

"We don't know what you mean."

"You must use your power to eliminate that which transgresses My world. Take this man and the tribe he leads. Destroy all else, then pray that this man can keep alive the life I gave his forefathers. Do not be afraid to do this. He is the only chance you have to realize your dreams. There will be many obstacles for this clan including Satan. Remember also that only these clans led by this man are beings with my breath within them. Everything else is simply the result of your folly. I give you this one chance now to make the transition to a world with hope."

The Father was gone. The pair never felt so desperate. Their mandate was clearly a reprimand. They felt the Fathers' frustration caused by transgressions against Him in all the realms of His domain. They could not fail Him. They must put an end to the life they started and bring it forth again within the confines of what is right and what is wrong.

"Yan, how do we do this?"

"We must use our powers."

"What powers?"

"The powers we have over the physical aspects of the planet."

"We have to kill everything using rain, wind, earthquakes, volcanoes and such?"

"Yes."

"That's gruesome."

"No more gruesome than what's been going on."

"How do we save the clan? You know they depend on the beasts."

"We will have to isolate the clan and everything they need to survive."

"Where?"

"We're going to have to wash away everything. It would be best if we could get the tribe to build a boat for themselves and all the creatures who would not survive a flood."

"Creatures…yes, all those except man."

"Right."

"So everything everywhere is washed to the sea except what's in the boat?"

"Right."

"That's a lot of water."

"Right again."

"So how do we get the tribe to build a boat big enough for this?"

"We'll have to get the mediator to contact the leader and tell him to build it."

"What's going to prevent the creatures from stopping him?"

"They're so caught up in their evil world they won't pay any attention."

"I know the animals are going to be a problem. How do you know the Father wants them to be a part of the new world?"

"The beings are the top of the chain, they can't survive without them. The Father has given the beings His breath of life, His approval to be. They are carnivorous. They depend on them as beasts of burden. They need them to separate themselves from the world that was. And they won't be a problem. Would you please contact the mediator? We must not delay."

"OK. I'll tell him what to do. I'm wondering if you'd like to take one last look before it happens."

"I don't think so, but I'll let you know after they've begun work on the boat."

"It's going to have to be a big boat. Are there any particular dimensions? I don't know. Tell him to count on divine guidance!"

"How's he going to get guidance from the Father?"

"He has come to his position through divine guidance. He will continue to receive it."

"You sound like nothing could stop him."

"Not with God the Father Almighty on his side. Now tell the mediator."

"OK. I'm gone"

Yin found the mediator in his usual place. He knew something big was going to happen. When Yin asked him to contact the beings, he was delighted.

"You want me to be the one to tell this man what he is to do? How do I do it?"

You simply put the thought in his head. At night when he's asleep, give him a vision of the destruction to come and the boat with himself on board. He should get the message."

"OK. I'll try right now."

The First Time

The man was inspired by the vision the spirit presented him. It meant the end of a lifelong battle to him. Finally there would be no more temptations from the creatures so much like him yet so different. He knew he was old and that it would require more work than he had ever done, but he knew he would be the first in a new world. He was proud and honored to be given the chance. All his life he had wanted this. He had taught his family that one day one of them would be given an opportunity to bring the spirit into the world again. He was thankful to play such a part. No sooner was the command given him until he set his whole clan to work on the boat. It was huge...as large a boat his clan could build in ten sets of the seasons. There were only a few of the lifeless creatures, cousins to the clan, who saw the boat. To them it was only the folly of the clan with the docile leader.

When the boat was almost complete, the man began to gather the animals in pairs. The boat could not be built which would house all the creatures of the land. The man had many decisions to make. He judged the animals by his own criteria. Only the best in a species would he saved. There were many species cousin to each other...again it was his judgment which pair in the group of species to allow the honor to carry on the strain in the new world. Every animal selected was given to the man. Somehow, when they were gathered together close to the boat and him, constant awareness of their place in the chain was alleviated. They no longer felt the fear of being a more dominant species' sustenance. All respected the right to live. They all ate plant life or fish which the man supplied plenty of. All the animals recognized the beings that gathered them together as the lucky ones they were to serve. They even saw them as the end of the chain. They envied their mysterious superiority. For the first time there was a desire to be free of their position in the chain but somehow too they recognized their duty to preserve their specie in order to provide the needs of all creatures...they were aware of their importance.

"Well, Yin, they're about ready. We need to figure out how we're going to do this."

"I've been thinking about this for a while now. I think the first thing will be to flood the area the boat is in to get it out safely to sea. As soon as they are out of the area we'll be getting the water from, we hit all land masses on the planet. This will be our last chance for you to relieve any instability in the crust. Do you think you can obtain a good stability?"

"Yes, there are few places with a lot of stress I've been holding back out of fear of disturbing the ecological balance. You're right about this being a good opportunity, but I can never get one hundred percent rid of the stresses that cause volcanoes, earthquakes and the like."

"How long would you be able to go without major problems?"

"Several millenniums."

"In that amount of time the beings should be spreading to other planets."

"Sure, if this works and the spirit of life the Father gave these beings is strong enough to win out over Satan, there's no telling what they could do with the physical world, not to mention their help in the spiritual world."

"I'll give them a couple of days of good strong rain. It should be a signal for the man and his clan to load the boat."

"Be sure and give them time to get all the animals on the boat."

"Don't worry about that. How do you feel about the destruction we're about to let loose with?"

"I think this is a case when the end justifies the means. If we are successful, I'm willing to do what is necessary. The life I'm about to destroy is life without the blessings of the Father. I knew from the day the bacteria evolved to consume algae, there would come the day I would have to put an end to the life that I convinced you there would be good to come out of and to let things evolve into something that would delight and honor the Father. Today is that day. The Father has guided us in bringing this about. I hope and pray all will turn out as would be ideal. I tell you now though; if Satan intervenes I will not give up. This planet is us. If it takes turning it back into a shimmering ball of nothing in His great universe, I will not let Satan spread from this planet. If these chosen beings fall prey to him, I will use all my power to destroy them too. They have been given the opportunity to live the everlasting life with the Father. This by itself is more than I would ever have imagined. We will soon destroy that which could never be a part of His domain. After all these years we come down to a boat holding all our dreams. If it means never realizing any of those dreams I will destroy also whatever comes of this mission. If it means life I allowed to exist going contrary to the Father's ways, I will never allow it to escape the confines of this planet.'"

"I'm with you all the way. Do you think Satan has a hold here? I don't sense that type of presence in any of the beings on the boat."

"I really don't think Satan knows about us. Surely this universe is too big for him to know our plans. The only ones who know we're here are the Father and the mediator."

"You don't think the mediator would betray us?"

"I hope he doesn't. We should pray Satan never gains control of him. Now what we must do is to keep the spirit alive in the chosen ones."

"It seems they're ready to begin their journey."

"That was just the right amount of rain...enough to signal the beginnings yet not so much to alarm the creatures to be left behind. Can you get them on their way?"

"Sure."

Yin drew a water spout from a tributary close by. Soon the boat was well out to sea. The couple used the most humane means they had to destroy life...the awesome power of water. Yan caused shifts in the crust to force up tidal waves and relieve the stress in the crust. The land mass, which had always been lopsided on the planet, shifted causing new continents and a better balance. The combination of earthquakes and water quickly did the job. Everything was washed to the sea or left to become the dust that allowed new life to spring forth.

The clan busied themselves taking care of the animals. All on board sensed their solidarity. There were really no problems except the anxiousness to begin again. When all the water had receded and the land masses settled into place, Yin and Yan brought the craft to land...Yan using currents, Yin a steady wind. Soon they reached land and the first thing that happened when the boat unloaded its cargo was that all gathered, beings and creatures alike, to pause and wonder with gratitude how it came to pass. It was the beginning of spring and seemed like the beginning of a new world...which, of course, it was.

"You know what all those creatures are going to be doing for a while."

"I knew you were going to say that."

"Say what?"

"Talking about the pleasures the creatures would have trying to repopulate."

"The beings too!"

"You know what the Father said about physical gratification."

"It can't be all bad if it's necessary to continue life."

"Remember when we were talking about manifestation as beings?"

"Yes."

The First Time

"Don't expect me to be your wife. You'd probably want to do that every five minutes, children or no children."

"I wouldn't be that bad. Don't you think we deserve a little physical pleasure after reaching this point?"

"Well everybody else is doing it. Why should we be different?"

"Where do you want to go?"

"Let's stay here so everyone won't forget we're the ones that started this beautiful mess."

"They don't know anything about us."

"That beats all. If it weren't for us they wouldn't be. We'll probably never get any recognition from them."

"Not that it's important, but don't give up on that yet. There's a lot ahead. Anything could happen."

"Do you have the energy left to strike up some lightning?"

"Coax it out of me."

"That's OK. I didn't really feel up to it anyway. You don't mind clear skies for a while do you?"

"If you're going to be that way I suppose I could use some drying out."

"You're not mad?"

"No. We both need to relax."

"I love you."

"I love you too."

The next few years were some of the best times there ever existed. All the creatures multiplied and assumed their positions in the chain. The beings increased their numbers too. The children were taught the ways of the Father and the spirit stayed alive and well. Just like many of the creatures, some of the chosen began to roam the land. Soon the desire to travel took the beings to many far away lands, some across the oceans. The old man died a peaceful death, knowing he had saved the breath of life he had been so privileged to be given.

"Yan, are you with me?"

"Yes, I'm here. What is it?"

"How do we keep tabs on everyone? They're so spread out."

"We'll just have to move about and check on them. As far as I've been able to tell, they all live with customs the Father would consider appropriate."

"Do you think this will last?"

"I'm very worried. We don't have much influence on them. If Satan discovers what the Father has in mind for them, he would never allow them a moment's peace. We'll just have to allow them to go on as they have been with hopes their spirit guides them through the temptations he will use to drag them into his world."

"Have you noticed the way the people of one location are developing different physical characteristics?"

"It makes you wonder if they'll ever stop evolving."

"As long as they never turn against each other, I'll be happy."

"That's exactly what Satan will try to make them do if he's given the chance. Right now the beings never give it thought ... good comes as the natural way. When Satan intervenes, he'll point out the alternative to the blissful way of life they have now. They will have a choice and some will reject evil, others will accept. When this happens, we will have the toughest battle we've faced yet."

"Is each being going to make the decisions by themselves?"

"I suppose there will come a time when the individual being will find Him part of society which dictates most of their choices. I think eventually the individual will have little say or power to affect their situations. When this happens, you know those who control the situation will be aligned with Satan because it is against the ways of the Father to dominate. I pray they never develop the power to annihilate an entire society, because if this ever happens, those in charge, those who follow Satan and try to perpetuate the circumstances of the chain, will never be able to put aside that kind of power. Of course if that happens, we will experience again what we've just been through. The only problem is we may not be able to save any beings, our dreams will be lost."

"Don't you think we could stop it?"

"I think, with time, the beings will have powers greater than ours."

"Could the spiritual world intervene?"

"You don't seem to understand. We don't have anything to worry about until Satan enters the picture. Even then, we'll have until they develop the power to cause worldwide destruction."

"Do you think we can keep the secret from Satan?"

"If he's still as crafty as he used to be, I wouldn't be surprised if he's already making plans to take over."

"Once he has control of an individual, can we ever get that person back?"

"Yes. They have a free will now. It's a matter of getting them to choose the Father's ways instead of Satan's. Then again you have the problem with perfection ... once you've transgressed against the

Father you would always remember the transgression. If a being cannot be comfortable that the Father will not hold against him his sins, then the situation will be hopeless in ever trying to get that individual back to the Father's side."

"How do we get them to understand the Father doesn't hold grudges? On the same line, if they have free will and Satan is so sure to step in with his influence, aren't we soon going to be fighting a losing battle?"

"It could turn out that way."

"Then we should go to the Father and ask for help."

"I think you're right. Have you consulted with the mediator lately?"

"No, but he comes by periodically to check on things. I'll put myself in the usual place and hope he comes soon."

"I get very lonely when you go to meet him."

"Then you come too. How would you like some gentle rain to help relax?"

"Beautiful. Can I get a small jolt or two of lightning?"

"Let's not get excited, we'll wash away our hopes."

The couple went and waited on the mediator, but he had decided there would be no cause for alarm any time soon. There wasn't. All the beings roaming the earth had plenty of everything they needed. Yin and Yan were very content to wait together every once in a while checking on the different tribes. They were proud of their world, but very anxious to discuss the strategy of defense for it from Satan. One day the mediator showed up.

"We thought you'd never show up."

"What's wrong?"

"Nothing in particular. We need to ask the Father how to protect our beings from Satan."

"That's not easily answered. Have you spotted evidence of his influence here?"

"No, not yet. We just want to be prepared."

"This is a subject I'd like for you to have the Master's own viewpoint on. We'll be back shortly."

It seemed only a few moments lapsed.

The Father returned and said "I understand you're worried about the devils' influence here. I am too. I anxiously wait the day I can take into my world the spirits developed here. But of course the only ones I can take will be those who choose my ways. When I gave them the breath of life, I gave them the option to follow My ways or not. Only I can know which ones are following my path. You two don't remember much of My world. It has been a long time. Before you left you never saw an instance where I was asked for forgiveness. Everyday now, I'm asked to forgive. Of course, I do, but only when there is a sincere desire to be a part of My world. I can tell you now that I will never again be able to open My world to an untested spirit. Few are the spirits that have never given in to the powers of Satan. I truly want for every one of the spirits created in this world to have the opportunity to be with Me forever. Of course this means alleviating the world of Satan. It may be early to tell you this, but this planet, and all the spirits that will come from it, may afford us in the spiritual world the opportunity to contain Satan in his own world. You realize what this would mean? If the plan works, you will know more than the satisfaction of being a part of it. Let Me try to explain. If these spiritual beings multiply, we have the source of an unlimited number of spirits to populate both my physical and spiritual worlds. Once Satan realizes this, there will be no end to the tactics he'll use trying to take over. The only recourse will be to teach the beings My ways. They should recognize what is and is not acceptable. You three know how simple it is. In order to do this I will send to all the different tribes one of the few pure spirits I have left. Of course they will come as one of the tribe. Hopefully, their teaching and example will give the spirit of these beings the will to stay with Me."

"I have finally completely separated My world, the spiritual domain you two chose to leave, from the world of Satan. Unfortunately, your domain, the physical world, does not lend itself to such separation."

"So this is what we have to work with. What will happen is this. We will compete with Satan for the spirit of these beings. When the spirit of these beings no longer has physical life to support them, the spirit will naturally enter the world it has chosen, either Mine or Satan's. Since the essence of a spirit will never change, I consider it safe to send My spirits back to your physical world. Here they can do some good. Since we will not venture into their activities until Satan's world is completely contained, all of our energy needs to be directed to the goal of ostracizing Satan from us."

"Are you saying the same spirit may live on the planet more than once?"

"I think some spirits may live here many times."

"And those spirits will not be prey to Satan."

"Once a spirit accomplishes the peace all spirits truly want, by following My ways, there will be no temptation great enough to cause that spirit to stray from Me."

"Aren't the spirits of these beings pure?"

"Yes."

"Then why not just take them into Your world now, and forget about exposing them to temptation?"

"I cannot do that because the bodies of beings that are not taken over by an existing spirit, is a domicile which creates a spirit. I need many spirits and bodies to fill this universe of Mine."

"You mean You want these creatures to leave the planet and inhabit other places?"

"Yes."

"You said You were going to send some of Your pure spirits. Did we know them and when will You send them?"

"You don't remember, but you did know them before your physical manifestation. I will send them when they want to come. They are all knowledgeable of the way Satan works. I'm sure they have their individual ideas as to how to fight his influence best. I doubt that any will want to come before Satan has made his move.

"Can You give any hints as to the activities You have in mind for after Satan is stopped?"

"The beings that have come into our midst are very creative and love life. I'm sure they will have an agenda. Another thing I wish to happen is the marriage of the physical and spiritual worlds."

"Is there anything we can do to help?"

"You've established a stable environment with beautiful transitions in the seasons. Simply continue these. Give them good times and bad. You'll be surprised how the weather will affect them."

"Something that's always bothered us...the beings slaughter of the animals for food. Will they ever be freed of the need for this?"

"There may be the time when they have to free themselves of this. Recently they lost many species in the chain. Fortunately, enough species survived to allow the chain to continue. The animals don't have a spirit. They are now just phenomena of the planet. The beings would be smart to protect them though, because it will be a very long time before they are not dependant upon them."

"How are Your spiritual domain and Satan's separated?"

"The worlds are radically different, and cannot exist together. It was simply a matter of separation. Now there will never be anymore mingling of the two."

"Will Satan send the spirits he has won over back to this world?"

"If he's going to put up much of a fight he'll have to."

"If there's going to be a way to contain him, why don't we just wait until the numbers of our spirits reach a certain level, and then allow Satan to destroy the world. We can contain him then and the planet will be open only to us."

"Two reasons...first, Satan is too smart, he knows we'd like to isolate him. That's why he will fight complete destruction. He'll always try to keep a foothold. Secondly, and most obvious, this species of life I've given spirit has come into the world through a process which will never be duplicated. If we ever let it die, it will mean the end of your dreams. Granted, eternity is enough time to find alternative activities for the spirits without the physical manifestation they enjoy the most, but whatever it would be it would not be the same. Something I should warn about now. If Satan realizes his doom, his ultimate revenge could come on his way out. At the time of his containment, the ability to destroy all life on the planet may exist. It will be up to us and the spirits we control to stop this from happening. Again, if we fail in this aspect, our dreams will be greatly curtailed."

"Father, are there any others like us...physically manifested in planets?"

"No. When your attempt seemed to fail, those who were going to follow suit, changed their minds. Then the split occurred, and we've been busy with it ever since."

"What is our role now, other then providing the weather?"

The First Time

"Actually the weather can take care of itself. You've been so good to Me; I'd like to let you decide your fates. You've been together so long I'd hate to see you split up now. As it stands, you have three options. You can come back to the spiritual world, remain here, or experience the pleasures of our new world as beings. Take time to think it over and take pleasure in being the only spirits to have this choice. Anymore questions before I leave you?"

"We'll hold them until we meet again. Thank you Father."

"Thank you. Goodbye."

"Are you prepared to do battle with Satan?"

"I don't like the idea of doing battle, period."

"We don't have much choice."

"I'll do it. I just don't like it. I can't imagine evil. I didn't like the food chain ... I thought that was evil and look what's come of it. The Father has even said it was not true evil, but actually a normal natural physical fact. There was no alternative for the life involved. Going against the Fathers' ways is a decision to upset the simple, beautiful, world the Father gave us. I can't imagine ever doing something that didn't seem to be the natural order of things.

"You chose to become physically manifested."

"The Father had always known the universe was ours. Before you and I chose to do it, the activities of the spiritual would keep us content. I don't remember, but I'd be willing to bet you and I simply became curious about this existence and decided to scratch our itch. Our decision did not go against the Father's ways. In fact I'd say the Father was at least inwardly pleased we chose to venture into his beautiful universe. And look what's happened. I think the Father is truly pleased.

Do you think the warnings He gave us about physical gratification is tied to Satan's influence?"

"Yes it must be. For example, sometimes I feel a desire to experience certain things such as developing and erupting a volcano. It's an experience I've never done just for the sake of doing it, and I know somehow I shouldn't, so I don't. But the desire is still there. On the same line, you and I get together and really create a ruckus because we like it. I don't think we're going against the Fathers way when we do that. Do you?"

"No. But if we were to turn our backs on our responsibilities to do that, it would be wrong."

"But we would never even consider that, would we?"

"No."

"I suppose it's those considerations Satan brings up."

"And more."

"Yes. We're going to be busy fighting him."

"It's too bad we can't get the Father's half of the spiritual world to help us out."

"Who said we couldn't?"

"How would they if they could?"

"The beings have spirit. I would think the Fathers' spirits could easily influence the beings."

"I'm sure the physical needs outweigh the spiritual in these beings. Don't you?"

"Probably, but they won't be totally immune to spiritual guidance. The Father is to send strong pure spirits to all the beings. I think we should give them a chance before we ask for the Father's entire world to revolve around ours. In fact, I don't think we should worry about anything until Satan shows up again."

"We should be watching for signs of his influence."

"You're right. Let's split up and observe the groups. Talk to you later."

"Bye."

The spirits spent several years. Not really understanding the way Satan worked, they were handicapped.

Somehow Satan had no problem infiltrating the tiny planet filled with susceptible spirits. It was no wonder that the planet quickly became the hope for all those who still remained with the Father. Likewise, it became the potential for sharp revenge against those in the Father's world that had cut all ties between those two worlds.

They were right though...the physical needs took precedent to spiritual needs. In several groups, which were restricted as to resources, the spirits saw early signs of a problem they would not see an end to for ages. In most cases, the groups had all the resources they needed, but there were isolated cases where this was not true.

"Were there any groups you observed that couldn't meet their physical needs?"

"Yes. One case in particular I saw could serve as a model for all the rest of the groups. This group chose to inhabit a small island. Like all beings they increased their numbers. It wasn't very long until the island couldn't support all of them. I feel that Satan was influencing them because instead of some of them leaving the island to seek more bountiful land, they all stayed. It wasn't long before they all were starving. To add to the problem, the overcrowding caused unhealthy conditions. Then they started quarrelling over resources and land. It didn't stop until there were only a few left to pick up the pieces. They've already begun to repopulate. I would imagine the same thing will happen all over again."

"Are you thinking the same thing I am?"

"If you're thinking that this will happen on a larger scale to all the tribes around the world in years to come, then yes we're seeing eye to eye."

"Do you think the spirits the Father will send can find a way out of this predicament?"

"I'm sure they will teach the beings how to avoid the turmoil the situation causes, but I don't think anything can help to change the situation. There will always be two choices. One will be Satan's, the other the Father's. The time will come when the decision will be for all the beings of the planet to make as a group. The Father wishes for the beings to go out and take their life into the universe. Of course Satan's way precludes all of that. The time for decision will come. They can choose to work together to tap the unlimited resources of the universe, or remain here and fight among themselves for the limited resources of this small planet. I have the feeling the Father will be patient to the point when it's a worldwide decision. Every being will vocalize their choice. Right now there's plenty of room for all. Eventually there will be enough beings to choose the Father's way and move into all the remote areas of the world. When there's no more room, it will be up to each individual being to use their influence in affecting the worldwide choice to do as the Father would wish them to do. The Father's spirits will come and teach His ways. But that is all they can do. They can't live the beings lives for them. Each being will be aware how every decision they make fits into the battle. You and I know Satan will be contained to this planet. Even if it means stepping aside and allowing him to have the planet, the nature of his ways precludes anything worthwhile coming of it. I only hope these beings, or the majority of them, will choose the Father's ways and reap the bountiful rewards He offers."

"Yan, do you understand how Satan is to be contained?"

"Not really. I have an idea though."

The First Time

"What's that?"

"The Father said, in the spiritual world, the two factions could not exist together. It was simply a matter of separating the two and now they don't mix. I have a feeling that some day the same type of thing will happen here. I suppose when the time comes that every being must side with either the Father or Satan in attempt to decide the fate of the planet. There will be those who judge or witness the beings' choice. When this has occurred, it will be possible to separate them according to their thoughts. I'm quite sure those who side with Satan will continue in their ways, thus destroying each other. It may be up to us to send the rest of them to their spiritual world. After that it's simply a matter of seeing to it that those who come into our world are spirits from our spiritual world or new spirits who will learn our ways. We just can't allow any of Satan's spirits the chance to escape the fate they chose."

"I don't understand how they will be separated."

"Some things I choose to leave up to the Father. I don't understand either."

"How long do you think we will have a purpose here?"

"Why?"

"I'd like to go back to the spiritual world."

"You don't want to become a being?"

"No. Not yet at least."

"Why do you want to go back?"

"I don't want to become a being and I'm tired of this planet. I'd really like to get in touch with the spiritual world again. I want to find out what other spirits are thinking. Maybe they can tell me more about Satan so I can be better prepared to deal with him when the time comes."

"Are you experiencing a need to get away from me?"

"Well we have been out here a very long time. Trying to keep ourselves occupied is getting old. Don't get me wrong ... I still love you as much as I ever did, and I still want our relationship to go on, but some time alone to reflect on our works and our relationship wouldn't hurt anything."

"You're right. I think you should go to the spiritual world. I'd like to change my situation too, but I'm afraid of locking myself into a situation as a being."

"Don't be afraid to come with me to the spiritual world."

"No. I want you to have some time for yourself."

"Thanks. Why don't you just stay here?"

"Things are boring here. I want to be a part of the action. I've always wanted to be a being. I think now would be a good time to do it."

"I'll wait on the Father with you. You should ask Him for some tips on how to save your identity when you become a being. I don't really like the idea of you starting out all over again with all that temptation around."

"Remember what He said. Now, once a spirit has accepted His ways and knows the peace they generate, it is very unlikely that the spirit would reject that to live in Satan's world of sin."

"What are you going to do if a female propositions you?"

"That's really not sin. What are you going to do if I proposition a female?"

"Oh damn you Yan."

"You don't really expect me to live the life of one of these beings and ignore one of the basic pleasures and duties they have."

"Well if you're going to be down here fooling around with women, it would just be fair for me to fool around too."

"Spirits don't fool around like that. I'm not trying to upset you. I would much prefer that both of us be a family on the planet. But you want time alone and I want to get to know the world we've created better. Becoming intimately involved with other beings is just a part of it. As a being I won't be aware of you. There will be nothing for you to be jealous about. The years will pass quickly and I'll be back with you. Just never forget how much I love you and that I'm doing this in preparation for battle with Satan."

"You're sure Satan can't seduce you into his world?"

"Yes. Don't worry about that."

"How long will you be gone?"

"For as long as I live as a being."

"I'll bet you don't even remember me when you get back."

"Please remind me if I don't."

"This is making me sad."

"Just think of all we've been through."

"Come with me."

"No, it's better this way. It will probably strengthen our relationship."

"Let's get the Father. He'll have to OK everything, and then make it happen."

"Is the mediator there?"

"He's always there lately."

"You two are going to 'fool around' on me aren't you?"

"Quit it Yan."

"I'm sorry. See if he'll get the Father for us."

"I'll be right back."

The father had been standing by. He knew the two would make their decisions soon.

"I take it you two want to change your situations."

"Yes, Father. Yin has decided she needs some time alone in Your world, so I've decided to see what life as a being is like."

"I told him I'd rather he come back with me, than to leave himself open to Satan's temptations."

"Yan won't have any problems with that."

"He says he's going to have relations with female beings."

"That's part of life for beings."

"I'm going to miss him."

"He'll be back with us before you know it."

"Even without a memory of my past life, there will still be something missing I won't find until my return."

"As we leave this domicile you chose as yours so long ago, and before you find yourselves in your new situations, I'd like you to look and see what lies in store for you and the descendants of the beings you allowed to exist. All of this will one day be at their disposal to do with as they please. The only confines will be their physical limitations and My ways. Sooner than you expect, these beings will face the easiest choices they've ever faced. Unfortunately there will be those among them who will make the wrong decision. There's nothing you can do for them. When the beings have separated themselves, I will give the treasures you see now to those who have chosen Me. The others will undoubtedly bring an end to themselves. Satan will rule only his spiritual world. Only I can permit the physical manifestation of spirits. The only way I will permit him into My world then would be reconciliation with Me. I will give him a chance, but that's all. Frankly, I don't expect him to change his ways. Perhaps some of those who follow him will sincerely change for their own good. I expect it will take only a short while for him to show his true colors and seal his fate of being locked away from these treasures. Only then can I feel at ease with Myself. I will offer him every opportunity to come to Me but the choice is his."

"Do you mean to say that after all the trouble he has caused and all the effort You've put forth to contain him; You're actually going to let him loose?"

"I will give him that one last chance."

"Do you think he will take good advantage of it?"

"I think it won't be long until he compromises his situation again and must be recaptured. The advantage of doing that though will be to regain many spirits anxious to repent."

"It always turns out that You have the most beautiful logic behind Your plans. Tell me, did You have all this planned out when You sent us to our home?"

"If I had to tell everything, what fun would it be to be the Father?"

"I must confess jealousy of a magnitude never to be equaled."

"I must confess My jealousy of you and your immediate plans.

Hopefully someday I too can experience the simple pleasures of life as one of the beings. Right now I'm a bit too busy for that. As a matter of fact I'm sure the spirits are missing Me now. Yin, just stay with Me. Yan go back to the world you've known for so long. You will be in a place very familiar to you. Wait there. All your memories will leave you as well as your sensory functions. After a while you'll find yourself in the womb of a good woman. The course of nature will supply you with life as a being. My blessings go with you. I expect good things from you.

"Keep a watch on me Yin."

"Goodbye. Come back safely."

"Thank You Father."

"Will he be alright?"

"Yes. And he will be good, but his mission is simply to enjoy himself. He's wanted to do this for a very long time. Many were the occasion he thought he could accomplish so much more than other beings if he had the chance. He will soon come to realize the life they lead poses problems daily. If he does nothing else, all I want for him is to experience the life he was so instrumental in bringing about. I hope he fathers a dozen children."

"Oh Father! How can you say such a thing in front of me?"

"How would you like to be the mother of those twelve children?"

"Are you serious?"

"I can arrange it."

"I haven't stepped foot in the spiritual world yet. I have a great need to return before I get involved in another adventure."

"I must warn you there are many spirits waiting for your return. They could spend years and years and never be satisfied of hearing of your adventure with Yan. You have only a little while to spend with them if you want to join Yan as his bride. How does it sound?"

"Again you amaze me. It must be nice to be so perfect."

"Enough is enough. Are you ready to be the guest of honor?"

"Yes."

"Let's go."

Yin was delighted to experience existence in the spirit world. As she was warned, the well-wishers and the curious were overpowering. As a matter of practicality, she gathered them all together and recounted her adventure. Even though it seemed she left nothing out, she spent more time answering questions than she did relating the story. Soon she became overwhelmed and thought how much more beautiful life as an infant being would be. The Father sensed her distress with being the most popular spirit in their world and came to her rescue.

"Are you ready to join Yan?"

"I'm certainly ready to get away from all this. I do miss Yan. Yes, I think I'm ready."

"You know you won't remember this, but don't be afraid. Yan and you will have a happy life. Satan won't be able to sway you. In fact he won't waste much effort."

"I was never sure I would enjoy life as a being."

"You'll like it if you aren't around much evil."

"Here I am, doubting a plan that Our Father the Almighty has in store for me. I'm very sorry."

"Don't be. I understand the nervous anticipation. Are you ready now?"

"Yes."

"Do you remember what I told Yan?"

"Yes."

"Then go with My blessings."

Yin and Yan were together again for their first temporary stay in the world they brought to fruition. Yan was the firstborn to a loving couple in a tribe wandering to find a land they could call their own. Yin was born to the family of a man who took most of the responsibilities as leader of the tribe. She had an older brother and two older sisters. The migration of the tribe was halted for only a day for each of the two births. There was nothing special about the infants. When the parents gathered to talk, there were comments on how unusually agreeable both the infants were. There were jokes that one day the two perfect babies would make babies of their own. It would turn out not to be a laughing matter.

Because of their ages and the small size of the tribe, the two were often put together so one or the other of their mothers could go about other business. Just as when they existed in a more bulky state, the two got along with few problems. They developed favorite games and played them hours on end.

It wasn't long before they discovered their sexual differences. Somehow it was not an amazing discovery for them. What would normally be a source of wonderment was simply accepted as fact. Their parents did not notice.

As the years passed, all the others in the tribe noticed the two. They were always together and they seemed to have an aura about them that generated kindness. They were kind to each other and kind to all the others in the tribe. This tribe was not virgin to Satan. Some of its members often went against the Father's way. Those who did always felt their shame more acutely when they saw the goodness the two surrounded themselves with. When they began the change into adulthood there were those among the tribe who felt a need not to allow their relationship to take over. There was a power associated with their goodness that was recognized, but not understood. It was a threat. Even though it was never said, their parents recognized the tensions and decided it would be best to separate them. They were very disappointed, but reacted as if they had known sadness all their life. Every time they saw each other their look indicated an unspoken resolve that someday they would be together again.

One day, without any discussion, the two saw each other and came together. Hand in hand they left the tribe. For whatever reasons, no one tried to stop them even though it was as if their most prized possessions were gone.

At first the journey for the couple was simply to escape the bonds of the clan they were born to. Of course it soon became a quest for a land. The spirit-filled beings were no different from the other beings with the exception of the fact that their spirit was uncut by the introduction of knowledge going against the Father's way. Yan killed other creatures only when it was absolutely necessary. Even then, every time he did, he prayed that one day those who would be his descendants would learn how to survive without slaughtering animals. He greatly appreciated Yin's compassionate look when he presented her his kill. The two used much less meat than any of the others they used to live with. They tried to eat as much plant life as they could, but of course during winter, their stores were lacking. For reasons unknown to them, they were always in awe of the weather. If it rained, they were puzzled. If it did not rain, they had the inclination to sit around and do nothing, just like the weather. When there was a thunderstorm, they found much comfort with each other. There was a new phenomenon for them to deal with. It came through the new undirected weather the planet now enjoyed. Since most beings knew well how to protect themselves from the elements, snow was not a problem for them. But for Yan and Yin, snow was something they could never get used to. For both, every time it snowed, it seemed as something was wrong. They were in awe to see it so beautifully cover every inch of ground. Often the occasion arose during a snow that Yan looked to Yin, and Yin looked to Yan, both with the same expression of fright. Of course there was comfort in being in the same boat, but that gave rise to inclinations that there was more in common between them than their history as beings provided them with. So on top of being perplexed by the strange weather phenomena, they were also perplexed by what they did not know about each other. They did not dwell on it though, having confidence that one day all would be explained. The two were happy with each other even if there was something missing.

It was during those cold days of winter the couple noticed Yin's rounding mid-section. There was an unspoken fear. Neither of the two had much experience with birth. They spoke of trying to find their old clan but quickly ruled it out. They had been able to overcome all of their obstacles before, now they would have to overcome this one.

By spring Yin was big enough that she soon tired of her daily chores. Yan would often do the work of both of them. Everything foreseeable they would need was gathered. The day came and there were no problems. The couple had a son. There were more than the usual feelings associated with the child. Again they could not be explained, but the child meant the fulfillment of age old dreams the couple could not understand, but knew were there.

The child was healthy and seldom cried. His spirit was virgin. The pair knew he would be like them. Life was good for the family. They stayed in the same place for many years. Eventually, there were a dozen children ... all living according to Father's ways. When the children came of age, their parents sent them forth to find their mates and teach the peace that comes with the Father. Most of the children found mates and chose to lead their lives as their parents ... away from Satan's influence. Yin and Yan saw their last child leave and began to feel their age as well as that special feeling that comes with the self-actualization associated with success at that age. They also felt their time on the planet should be coming to a close. After a few years alone, a very harsh winter came. In the snow with which once they eliminated many species, they found their own deaths. Once again they found themselves in the company of the Father in His Spiritual world.

"So tell Me, how is life as a being?"

"Are you speaking to both of us?"

"Yin, you haven't told him yet?"

"We've just come back. I didn't know how to explain."

Yan responded "We've just come back; I think I'm owed an explanation."

"Indeed you are Yan. After you made your decision to become a being, and I had you on your way, I asked Yin if she would like to be your mate. I did this to save you from becoming involved with a woman who knew Satan's ways. I hope you aren't upset. I assure you I had only your best interest at heart."

"No Father. I'm not upset. In fact, I feel as though I knew something was up all the time ... Yin made a different kind of woman. I was glad to have her. Our children were lucky to have her as a mother. They were never exposed to Satan and his ways until they left our care. Even then they rejected Satan and chose the peace of living with their mates away from beings who knew Satan's ways. I look forward to seeing how many generations of my descendants will know only Your ways. I'm very happy Yin came to be my wife."

"Yin, I know you feel like you pulled one on me, but don't feel bad. I'd hate to think what I could've gotten into if you had not been there."

"I was thinking you wanted to be alone."

"I was thinking you wanted to be alone here."

"I did, but every spirit here wanted to know what we'd been through. I wanted solace and ended up not having any time to myself. When the Father suggested I go to you, I had reservations. I didn't want to interrupt your adventure, but after all I thought the Father knows best. Of course I came to you. Now I love you more than ever, but I don't want to encroach upon you. You've always been strong with me, such as the time you made me promise not to interfere with the life on our planet. Its times like that I fear now. I'm sure there will be times I want to interfere, but won't, and I'm scared of that too."

"Don't ever be afraid to speak your mind with me. I value your opinion as much as I value you. Like you say, I'm sure too the times to come will have as much or more hard times for us. I'm sure you see as I do, that we are becoming an entity. I'm not afraid of that. I pray you will continue on with me."

"For some reason, I feel inferior to you. I don't know what lies in store for us. How can I say I will go on with you with these issues facing me?"

"You and I are on equal ground. I know no more than you about what lies in store for us. This issue of you feeling inferior to me must have some roots. I don't understand, but I hate it. I sense you feeling inferior to me, and that interferes with me turning to you when I need you. Father, can you tell us why this issue exists?"

"It's a problem as old as you are. Your spirits have a past which for the most part has been forgotten with time. Often I've thought to bring up the past to all My spirits, but then I stop and see the differences among them, and all of a sudden, I see the beauty in them. I don't want to erase the differences they've caused in each other. Now, seeing you two adapt your differences to the differences in the beings, I wouldn't change a thing. You see when I created you I started with one spirit. It was magnificent. It and I lived together happily for a length of time you wouldn't understand. We both knew it couldn't last forever though. It asked Me what would be something it could do to please Me and yet still bring to a conclusion the beautiful existence we knew would have to come to an end. I told it if we had to bring our relationship to an end, I didn't want a void, I'd want more of it. Neither of us could see how to do that. Then out of frustration, it began to define itself as to location. Then, when it realized itself as one entity, it took itself within itself. Of course it had to come out of itself and so from the top and bottom of where it had gone into itself it emerged as two with nothing lost and nothing leftover. The two spirits were exactly the same. I loved it, but it was gone. I was left with two. Each spirit was the same and with the same characteristics as their predecessor. The only difference was they had each other as well as Me. I'm sure you can imagine the competition for My attention as well as the struggle for their identity. Well they found it. You two come as descendants of those two. You are both equal in every way, but inevitably you'll point out some type of difference. For instance, your gender was established years ago as a means to an identity. It's been a cute game over the eons, but as I said, I'm tempted to recall the past, as I have for you, and put all back on the same ground."

"You mean all of us are the same?"

"No. The prime example would be you two. All the other spirits here are envious of you. It's the cumulative effect of experience that makes a spirit what it is."

"When did gender come into it?"

"Soon after it split, the two spirits took on characteristics all their own. This basic difference will never be alleviated no matter how the spirits change."

"Is there a tie between our gender and the gender of the beings?"

"You are well aware of the development of the beings. It was a process of natural selection for them to be in the position they are now. It was fate that they offer My spirits natural domicile with genders compatible with the gender of the spirits. I'm very pleased the way things turned out. Imagine asexual creatures such as worms as the end of the chain. I'd doubt you'd have kindled any interest in the spirits to become worms."

"Did You influence the chain to select the beings so they would be the perfect creature for us to have as our means of physical manifestation?"

"Let Me remind you that I have created all, including you. If there's something you don't totally understand please just accept it as reality. As I have let you know before, I am very grateful of the role you and Yan have played in creating the world of the planet. Both of you, I consider as very special among your peers. You've been instrumental in creating a world which has become the focal point of the universe. There is not a spirit here that hasn't considered life as a being. A large part of the population here is anxious to experience the physical world. There is a slight problem though. All you spirits have always been anxious to be different. Physical manifestation as a being surely provides this. Another way for you all to differentiate yourselves is to do the things I don't allow. I have no problem controlling those urges here in My world, since I cast out Satan and his followers. Already he has taken over your planet so how can I turn all My spirits loose down there? Why should I put them to the test? Better yet, how do I get back what I hoped would be the birthplace of My new world, the world brought about by the marriage of My spiritual world and My universe?"

"Please. We certainly mean no disrespect but, don't you have some type of plan to accomplish these things?"

"I have My ways. It is certainly an insult from those who don't follow them; there is no true life without them. The problem is getting all My spirits to realize this. Most spirits, who have turned to Satan, never gave their decision the proper consideration. Those spirits will be begging to rid themselves of Satan's cursed way of life. Right now we face an influx of spirits thanks to your efforts on the planet. I'm sure most of them will prefer to continue on as a being in that world...which is fine. The spirits here want their turn at physical manifestation. What must be done is to give all the spirits, who are beings, guidance. This guidance will come from Me through spirits I know will succeed in example, leadership, and command. Hopefully, the majority of beings will follow them. I must warn you now that the day will come that I will have My world back. Satan and those who follow him will exist only in their spiritual world and I will not be in a hurry to free them from that grisly world. I will have My world for many years before I give them their chance to prove they accept My ways."

"What we need to do here right now is decide your destiny for the immediate future. I would think you've had enough of the planet for a while. I wish you'd stay here with Me at least long enough to get re-orientated to this world. I hope one day the society of the planet will closely coincide to the society we have here. Of course they are two different worlds, but you'd be surprised how well they could parallel each other. Ultimately, they will merge, but of course that will be a long time in coming. It would be so nice if we could quickly overcome Satan, but I'm afraid it's going to take a long while."

"I would never try to second guess You so I'd like to ask Your opinion about us. We have always been close, even before the days of our physical manifestation. How do you feel about us as an entity?"

"I look at you two and see the pair of spirits I was left with after My lone spirit decided it must share Me. Just as they produced more spirits, you have produced more spirits. And in turn they will produce more spirits. You can now understand that no one spirit can do Me any good, with the exception of the first spirit whose most glorious act was to end itself for your sake. You can also see the evil of a spirit working for its own glory in Satan. For you two to consider yourselves as an entity is as I wish for all the spirits. This doesn't mean I wish for all spirits to pair off. I just want every spirit to realize they are not alone, and that there is a responsibility to interact to bring about those things they know I want to be. On the planet, the pairs of spirits begetting more spirits know their responsibility lies in rearing their young to follow My ways so that one day all spirits, with no exception, will have their place in the universe. Of course the rewards will be appropriate to their deeds. Let me tell you now that you hold a very special place with Me. I consider you impervious to evil. Your place with Me is secured. The decision I ask you to make now, is a decision that will last for eternity. Every moment of your life the decision will be "What next?"

"Because you're impervious to evil you may entertain yourselves at will. When you tire of the spirit world, the physical world awaits. Your every wish is reality. I'm sure though that in so much as this concept is appealing, I know you wish to remain involved in My serious affairs. I am, of course, pleased to see this. Your common experience will never be duplicated. There will be few spirits given the opportunity equal to that you've sought out for yourselves. Even fewer will be those who realize this opportunity and execute their actions to accomplish the marvelous deeds that are possible. If you're suddenly feeling a sensation of elation because you think luckily you've overcome and championed the challenge that will be the most ominous in your life, then savor and remember this moment. Let this moment become a part of you. You deserve this. You deserve to recall this moment at will. This is a unique part of you that no other spirits will have to call upon. This experience makes you great spirits. If you never accomplish anything else during your life you can always remember this moment and you as spirit will shine as bright as any other spirit. As I said you are free to do as you please. I would appreciate a close tie with you. What would you like to do now?"

"Yin, we know each other so well, may I speak for us?"

"Yes."

"Father, the memories we have are primarily since the time of our physical manifestation, on the planet. We've been together, yet alone since then. For a while at least we'd like to be together and alone in the spirit world. Unless You have something pressing for us to do now, we'd like to take our leave and return when we feel the priority of worldly affairs take precedent to the obligations we have to each other as an entity."

"This sounds like an idea coming from strong forthright spirits.

Take all the time you like. Feel free to come and observe before you become involved here again. That would allow you to forego unnecessary commitment in a situation we really don't need you. Take time to discover your powers. Take pleasure in your world. One thing I ask you not to do just yet, would be to become physically manifested anywhere without My knowledge. I'd hate to lose you again like that. Besides we're still in the infancy with your planet, and it's keeping us plenty busy, we may need your help. One thing you may like to do would be to scout out planets and find one you'd like to call your own, for the time we decide the universe should be open to spirits for habitation as physical beings."

"You're talking about the time when Your spiritual and physical worlds are merged?"

"They are merged now to a certain degree, but yes, I'm talking about the time when they are inseparable, when all beings are conscious of both aspects."

"But you say that will be a long time coming."

"Everything is relative. Yes, it will seem like a long time. But it will not be near as long a time as the period beginning with your manifestation to your return here after your life as a being."

"Then we should stay aware of time during our sabbatical?"

"I'd say for you to do the things you need to, but not to forget what else is going on."

"Yin, are you ready?"

"I'm anxious to go and get back. I don't want to miss any new developments."

"Then this is good bye. We thank You."

"Do Me one favor as I see you off. Recall the feeling I asked you to commit to memory, and let Me see you shine."

The couple did recall the pleasure that would be theirs and only theirs for eternity. They went to an out-of-the way area, far from the other spirits in the Fathers spiritual world. The first thing on the agenda for the couple was to discuss their relationships. The most important topic dealt with the fact that the relationship was not preconceived. Their closeness in the beginning may have given warrant to discuss a planned relationship, but it did not happen that way. They were thrown together and dealt with each other. They struggled with their circumstances and together, brought life to a planet. Then they experienced the life they made possible. Almost accidentally they became an entity. The first topic of discussion was to recognize and deal with that fact.

"If you had known what was to have happened, would you have avoided it?"

"If I had known we'd be here discussing in hindsight as we are, our accomplishments, surely I would have done everything I did just to be here with you having this beautiful conversation. And I can confidently say that you feel the same way."

"I don't think I'll ever feel as good about anything as I do about being here alone with you. We look behind and see how we reached this point, and then look ahead to see what lies in store. Then we feel each other and without reserve there's the contentment of finally knowing there will never be the question of whether we belong together.

"Could what we've done, been preconceptions of life?"

"We'd certainly be good witness to living without preconceptions."

"Over the years it hasn't been routine for us to acknowledge our love by simply stating the fact. Why isn't that important for some reason?"

"It's because we both recognize that, this most beautiful experience of self actualization as a couple, has a prerequisite of love.

The First Time

Everything we've ever done that we can remember has depended on our love for each other. I hope from now on you never question whether I love you. Whatever the consideration, know that I love you. I've found it rather simple to rely on your love. After many steps, you finally trust the ground will support you."

"We're different."

"We're one."

"Nothing will change that?"

"Would you ever allow it to change?

"I can't foresee the future."

"Then I suppose nothing has changed. You're still insecure with me, and I will always have to show you my love is always there. Don't think that's a problem ... I certainly don't mind reassuring you that I do. But put me on record now...if there's ever a time when you're not sure, or I'm not there to reassure you, I urge you to accept on faith that I love you and always will."

"Thank you. That relieves a lot of tension."

"Did you really think I resented the way we've come to be?"

"Until now, you never said to dispel the doubt I might have had."

"I'm glad that's over with. Do you know what I'd like to do now?"

"Normally, I would say you wanted to make rain or babies, but spirits don't do that."

"The day will come when they do!"

"It will be nice. What do you want to do now?"

"The Father has graciously given a blessing allowing us to recall, as we first experienced it, the memory of being with Him and realizing the cumulative effects of our lives. Part of the magic of the memory is being together to recall it. It wouldn't be the same to recall it alone...that would only produce a void. Now since we realize how we feel about each other it should have an even more beautiful meaning. For a while let's recall it to remind us who we are."

"We're beautiful, aren't we?"

"I think it's time we make the dignity we've gained a permanent part of us, instead of recalling those feelings when we feel we need it."

"Wouldn't the Father have us do that if it were a good idea?"

"Sure, I'm not saying we should make the feelings a permanent part of us. I just think we should start realizing what we've done and carry ourselves accordingly."

"I like the old you."

"I like the old you too, but we've come to a new position. We should radiate an aura appropriate for who we are."

"I think humility is noble."

"If we're to be an example to the other spirits we should show pride to be who we are."

"Yes. An aura of superiority is not what I am and would prevent me from communicating that everyone involved in accomplishing the Father's goals deserves the same respect we do."

"You're right. I suppose I've been a bit vain."

"Anyone who's done what you have has a right to consider vanity. Our position is secure. That alone, sets us apart. I must admit though … if it weren't that I'd be afraid of loosing the Yan I love, I'd probably help create an aura as radiant as the mid-day summer sun in a white desert."

The First Time

"The idea was appealing wasn't it?"

"Yes. Just for our sake we should shelf the idea. Someday we may get bored and decide to try it anyway."

"OK."

"How do you feel about the idea of a new planet?"

"I'll always be attached to our first, our home."

"Are you open to finding one just for us?"

"A hiding place wouldn't be a bad idea. It would be nice if we could find one similar to ours ... that way we would know how to bring it life. Perhaps we could find one that would sustain the life we've already begun."

How would we transfer life?"

"If life is to spread throughout the universe, there must eventually be a way to transport it from our first home to the different places it is meant to go."

"I think we must be overlooking something. Don't you think the Father will merge the spiritual and physical worlds before the life on the planet begins to fill the universe with its life?"

"I don't know. I think the beings are capable of great things, including escaping the confines of the planet. The only problem is that the Father will not allow Satan to roam from the planet. So it will have to be after the time the spirits who follow Satan are separated from those who follow the Father's way when the universe will be open to His spirits. The complete merging of the spiritual world and the physical world will also come after that time. If I had to guess, and I do, I would say the merger will happen before there's much relocation in the universe."

"Yan said you thought the beings will be capable of escaping the confines of the planet. Do you think they'll try relocation before the merger?"

"The technology they discover will probably be used by the beings that choose to relocate. If the merger is as I conceive it, the beings will be aware of life in the spiritual realm, but of course they will still be bound by the laws of physics. This is why it is so important for them to develop the technologies that will give themselves a free hand to use the resources and space the universe makes available. There's nothing to worry about though, because even if the beings master the technology that will be used, the way of Satan will preclude anyone from using it for the glorious purpose it is intended. Just as the island tribe refused to leave their island to escape the evil associated with staying there, those beings aligned with Satan will use the technology to further Satan's fight to control the planet. So again, we'll have to wait for the end of that world as we know it before there's a true union of the planet with its universe."

"I wish I knew how the separation will happen."

"One thing I strongly believe is the Father will give the beings every chance to make good of their situation. The spirits he will send to them will show the way. There will not be one being who can claim ignorance after they have completed their mission. As the Father said, they may have many lives as beings to prove themselves. Those who have one life could be judged simply by that life. Those who are not on the planet at the time of judgment will be in the spirit world they have chosen. The judgment will be simple. The spirits who show the way will return to each and every being and by simply being with them, they can judge by their thoughts which way they have chosen. Again you see how easy it will be to make the separation. Those who belong to Satan will continue in their ways to bring about their destruction. Those who follow the Father's way will save themselves by alienating themselves from evil. If there are any killed who would not have otherwise been killed, they will return to the Father's spiritual world where they can request new physical life as all the Father's spirits will be able to do."

"Then there will be life everlasting for those on the planet."

"Yes, and for those in the Father's spiritual world also. On top of that, the spiritual world will become a part of life for the beings. There will be nothing to hinder them. They may swell their population because they will not be confined to the planet. The universe will provide ample resources and space. Many will leave the planet, find another one and create the world of their dreams. Later, they will travel to and from worlds of such variety that one could travel forever and never tire of meeting new beings and diverse experience."

"Do you think the Father is simply offering us a head start?"

"I think it's more than that. He must realize we need our independence. We've become accustomed to it. Also we would be capable of creating a world we would enjoy. Of course we'd have to have technology to execute our plan, but we're the only ones now that know it's there waiting to be brought to life. All we have to do is dream, bide our time, and we can be the leaders of the exodus. We can show everyone, physically embodied spirits and pure spirits, what is possible."

"And you're sure that's what the Father would like us to do?"

"We can always ask, but I think it would be best to make a proposal of it. Would you go along with that?"

"We just concluded that one of the reasons He suggested we find a place was to allow us some independence. Now you're saying we should share our new world with everyone."

"We can't accomplish much on our own as spirits or beings. I'd be willing to give up the first world we created if it would allow the technology we need to make the spheres of the universe inhabitable for beings. Later we use the technology we bring forth to create an abode for ourselves, one we would ask the Father to make our own."

"Then we need two spheres; one to be used as the first stepping stone into space, another as one we would use as a home."

"Let's make it more than a home. Let's make it capable of traveling throughout the universe so we can visit all the worlds that will spring forth."

"That's a good idea, but I'd like it to be able to support the life we helped start."

"What else?"

"We should be able to imitate any type of weather we'd like."

"We should have all technology at our fingertips."

"We're getting a lot of people involved here."

"That's OK. We'll use a large planet so we'll have room for them and us both."

"But then how could we call it our own?"

"I'm sure that all the beings and people traveling with us will someday want a place of their own. Then I'm sure we'll replace those who leave with others who would like the experience we would offer."

"I suppose you're right, but what about us?"

"We'll be beings then and our needs will be few. A simple residence will suffice for us."

"This all sounds pretty nice. You want to find the Father and run it past Him?"

"Maybe we should find the spheres we'd like to use."

"I'd feel better if we had His approval before we lay claim to any planets. I'm still not sure I like the idea of having other beings around on the sphere we call our own."

"Do you know what 'life everlasting' means?"

"Sure."

"What?"

"Forever, eternity."

"Right. Don't you think in that frame of reference there will be plenty of time to ourselves? We owe a debt to the spirits we left behind when we became the planet and also to the spirits we've helped to create. I feel it's wrong to be thinking of ourselves right now."

"You're right. We need to stop and make a game plan. We'll be with the Father soon. We need to know what we want to do. Would you like to pick out a planet we can use as the stepping stone?"

"That's one thing to do."

"What else?"

"We need to see to it that the beings are still making progress in mastering their environment."

"I'd like to see if we can get the spirits excited about the future. I know that really won't accomplish much, but most of them are understandably forlorn about what's happening."

"That's a good point."

"So first we find the planet, and then we talk to the Father. If He says OK, we talk to the spirits. Then go to the planet and give our legates a progress report."

"Do you have any ideas on choosing a planet?"

"Let's make it the same galaxy."

"OK. What else?"

"If we're going to have such advanced technology to use, we don't need anything other than a relatively stable planet."

"This is going to be easier than I thought."

"Let's make it relatively close but not as close as possible."

"Why not make it a whole solar system?"

"Fine. Variety is the spice of life."

"That's really all we need to know. All we need to do now is check out a few stars and find one with at least two stable planets."

"Let's go. You lead."

"Ready?"

"Yes."

"Stick with me."

The expedition did not take long. Most of the systems they found met their criteria. They felt it an important choice so they ended up using a game of chance to make the final decision.

"We should name this place."

"Here we go again."

"What are you talking about?"

"You are trying to pick out names?"

"Fine! You pick it out."

"Es."

"You can't be serious. Sooner or later this place will be the hope for millions of beings. How did you come up with that?"

"It fits. Besides, you left it up to me. You will have to come up with something better or the name remains Es."

"Well, I'm going to think on it."

"Don't come to me in an eon or two with a new name."

"I'm going to give it some thought."

"Fine. Take all the time you like. But when we talk to the Father I'm going to call it Es. I like it. You're going to have to come up with something extra special to beat that."

"Why do I have the feeling that name is permanent?"

"Because I feel you're about to give in and let it be permanent."

"You win."

"I love you."

"Fine. She loves me because I just let her name the threshold of the universe a name you have to repeat three times to hear. Not that you can't hear it, it just doesn't register."

"Let's go find out what the Father thinks."

There was only a short wait for them to see the Father.

"Father, we would like to become involved in the future of the beings."

"How so?"

"By aiding their efforts to leave the confines of the planet. They will eventually have the technology to do that. We would like to help them."

"When was the last time you checked the situation on the planet?"

"Neither of us has visited since we left."

"Are you aware of the factors that must be overcome before I will allow any of them to leave the planet?"

"Yes Father, but the beings were making good progress in discovering the laws of nature. It shouldn't take too long before they have the capabilities to leave."

"They won't develop capabilities until they need them. The time they will need them will be the time the population is swollen on a world-wide basis. This will not happen until they stop trying to dominate each other through warfare, and that won't happen until those who go against Me are separated and rooted out. Even after that, the priority will be to merge My spiritual world and My physical world. After the merger My guidance will allow many more spirits to live on the planet than before. Yes, one day there will come the desire for the spirits to fill the universe but that will be a long time in coming. Tell Me. What were your plans concerning the departure from the planet."

"We were interested in showing others that it could be done. We even went so far as to pick out a planet we thought suitable to be the threshold."

"Tell Me about it."

"There's not much to tell. It's in the same galaxy for convenience. Actually we picked a whole solar system. We've name it Es."

"I like the name. Will any of its planets support life?"

"With the proper technology."

"I presume you will leave it up to the beings to produce the technology?"

"Yes Father."

"My advice to you two is not to play a waiting game. You are both great spirits. You have a unique perspective of the past. You can look back over the eons to see the progress of the beings and relatively speaking, it won't be long until the time we conquer evil and begin anew. We are all anxious. Naturally, waiting out this interim period will make it seem like an eternity. I had hoped you would search out a planet you could enjoy as in the early days of the home you've provided us. I can understand why you've come back to Me with plans for the beings. One day you will see your plans come to fruition, but it will take time. Now we need to decide on your activities for the present. To avoid the same mistake, I think you should be involved with the beings. Much has happened since you returned to Me last. It is time to begin sending spirits to be physically manifested as beings to point the way to life with Me. I know you two are an entity in yourselves, that's why I hesitate to offer you the responsibility. Do you see a position of responsibility I can offer you as a couple?"

"Yin, do you know of anything we can do?"

"Correct me if I'm wrong. These spirits would be manifested in the same way as we were manifested as beings. They will need parents who will foster and promote Your ways. Ideally, they will know the role of their child."

"If such a family situation could be created, it would be much better than sending a spirit into the world by itself."

"You must plan to send many spirits to different parts of the world. Will you send them all at the same time?"

"No. I think we should learn from each time we send a spirit the factors it will have to deal with and how to overcome the problems

Stephen J. Burns

of the world."

"How many will you send?"

"Just enough so that every being is afforded the opportunity of life with Me. Of course every spirit I send will establish its own path. It won't be realized until close to the time of the merger that all the paths lead to the same destination. Until that time, there will be many who insist there's only one road to this world. Of course the spirits will build into their guidance principles objections to other systems of guidance. But ignorance of other systems will cause some friction until close to the merger. It will come to light that these different approaches result in the same end."

"Have you sent anyone yet?"

"Not on this mission."

"Perhaps you would allow us to act in the role of parents to one of these spirits."

"Let me consider it for a while. Since you don't want to be alone, I'd like you to spend some time with other spirits here. It won't be long. I think it would help you to realize who you are. I hope their questions don't wear you out. I'll be with you soon."

"Thank you Father."

The couple joined the other spirits who surprised them. The spirits who were not allowed to become human beings had developed their powers. They learned to visit the planet and observe as spirits. Every one of them had formulated an idea of how to live on the planet and not transgress the ways of the Father. All were very anxious for the time they could put their plans into action. From first hand experience the couple told them it was not as easy as it seemed. They warned them that becoming physically manifested as beings causes one to lose all memory of the spiritual world. The spirit retained its basic nature, but the trials associated with being a

[141]

human were great, and temptation was always present. Their advice was to wait until both worlds were merged and temptation was gone. The reaction was negative. Most said the sooner the better. When they learned the couple had plans to become human again, the spirits were puzzled. The question, of course, was why the couple was afforded opportunities they weren't. The answer was fear, but few found consolation in the reasoning of being protected. They survived the schism, their spirit was strong. They were ready to fight for the Father.

"All of you are prepared for battle?"

There was no response but all had mixed emotions of restrained determination and guilt. The words coming from the Father made them all realize the power of Satan and the Wisdom of the Father.

"You realize now why I haven't allowed you to go to the planet. Now you are pure. I will not allow you the test. Remember what eternity means...there will be plenty of time for your life as beings. Consider one second in an hour as the time since Yin and Yan first became manifested as the planet. Take another second for the time it will take to secure it for worthy purposes. I know this is difficult for you to understand, but it is so. I am happy to see you concerned for the destiny of the planet and the beings that inhabit it. Many of you found your beginnings there. What I am concerned with is that in all the preoccupation with being physically manifested you forget the pleasures of this world. It didn't use to be that way. It used to be that you would occupy yourselves with each other and the beauty of the universe. I would like to see you rekindle those pleasures. I would be very happy to see all of you prepare for the next "few seconds." Get to know each other. Pair off. Go together to find a place in the universe. Stop worrying about this interim. It will pass."

"Excuse me Father. Do you really want all these valiant spirits to stay here away from the situation?"

"I have sent spirits who will lead the beings to Me. These spirits, those who have been with Me and those who come from the planet and are worthy to stand with those who have been with Me, need not prove themselves. They need not be exposed to Satan's temptation."

"Isn't Satan sending his spirits back to the planet to seduce more into following him?"

Silence.

"Forgive me my ignorance. I realize the time will come soon enough that the planet is Yours. I can't understand your willingness to allow Satan to be fought by a chosen few. There are many spirits here anxious to save those who might be lost to Satan."

"Stop and change your perspective and you may understand. Imagine Me with one spirit and the universe, or Me and the universe, or just Me. Then look at these spirits. Then look at the world you were so instrumental in bringing to light. Then think of eternity. Wouldn't you be a bit wary about putting all these beautiful spirits in jeopardy? Wouldn't you rather pity spirits who choose evil by allowing them to follow their chosen paths instead of risking spirits that have proven their righteousness to go after them?"

"I hate to see any spirits lost to Satan."

"There will be a time for them to have a second chance, but they will never know the pleasures you, these spirits, and those who seek Me before the time of judgment will know."

"What if Satan is successful and takes over the planet?"

"I thought you realized that evil will never succeed. There may come the time when it is in the dominant positions of course, but then it will die of its own inherent weakness. Satan will retreat to his world. Then those who remained faithful to Me will inherit the planet and bring it and the universe to fruition."

"When will the merger take place?"

"When Satan and those who follow him are contained to their own world. Do you have anymore questions?"

"No Father. Wait! Yes Father. What about the spirits who will show the way?"

"I've sent several, but few developed much of a following. I was sad to lose one I hoped would be very strong to Satan. I will send more."

"When a spirit follows Your way, You bring the spirit here. When the spirit follows Satan, the spirit goes to him and is usually sent back to seduce more spirits to his world. What about those who do not prove themselves one way or another?"

"They are afforded the opportunity to decide. They are sent back to the planet. I will only allow those into My spiritual world who I know are beyond reproach. So in essence, I am filling My world with those who will live with Me forever, and the rest are sent back to the planet to let their true nature show. On the last day for Satan to influence the world only those who actively and willingly follow his ways and recruit others to his world will be caught. Those who follow My ways will take over the lead. Those in the middle will no longer have Satan's temptation and will naturally support My spirits showing how beautiful life can be."

"What's happening on the planet now?"

"If you'd done as I asked you, you would be able to find out for yourself. Just about all the spirits here can show you how to visit the planet and observe. I leave you now."

"Thank You. Goodbye."

"What do you think Yin?"

"I think we should observe the beings the same way the other spirits here have been. Then we can see what the beings are facing. After that we will know how to help a spirit sent by God in providing the beings with life compatible to the Father's ways."

"Are you ready for motherhood?"

"Not yet, but I will be."

"Let's go."

The couple sought advice from many of the spirits. They found that by thinking of a situation on the planet they put themselves there. If the spirit was not familiar with a situation on the planet it could simply be with another spirit who did and both of them would transport themselves there. Once they were there they could go anywhere on the planet.

Most of the spirits had found situations they kept up with. After visiting certain humans so many times, the spirits became attached to them rejoicing in their triumphs and suffering with them the tribulations of life on the planet.

The couple was amazed to see how things had changed. The beings had formulated languages and set the languages to the written form. They no longer roamed in groups for the sake of finding food. They had learned to grow their own food and raise animals. There were many systems used to determine social status. They had learned many things which helped deal with the weather related elements. The rules of etiquette had changed greatly.

The questions that had always bothered the beings were still there though. The basic questions were: Who am I? What am I to do? Who do I owe my existence to? If there is more to this world than I have as my tangible environment, where is it?"

It was those questions the couple would have to answer. Beyond that, they knew God, and that knowledge would have to be given to the beings accurately. There were many beings who answered the basic questions wrong and were astray from the truth. Every society they studied had its own setup, but none were aligned with the

Father's ways. The old principle of dominate or be dominated, was still in effect. The couple did not want to accept the fact that Satan ruled the world, but they could not see an end to that until judgment day. They decided the most effective approach would be to concentrate on saving the individual's spirit. They remembered the Father's stance: Why send righteous spirits after bad ones. All the beings had free will. They had to choose between the Father and Satan everyday. The couple made a pact to the effect of somehow showing the majority of spirits the way of life that would allow them into God's Kingdom, and when the time came that the Father would give those who did not choose the path to His Kingdom a second chance, they would be there to help them any way they could. "Do you think we're ready to raise a child that can help the beings?"

"Yes. Let's get an audience with the Father."

"I am with you now!"

"Father, why is it lately You're always around when we need You?"

"I know your needs."

"Then You know we need to do something positive to help out the beings."

"Yes."

"Do You have a spirit that we can help do Your bidding on the planet?"

"No. It's not time for that yet."

"What do You mean?"

"You two will have to be born into that world and join yourselves as a couple before I can give you a child."

"That makes sense."

"When we're ready, You will send us a great spirit...won't You?"

"Yes. I'll do that."

"Then it's time for us to become physically manifested again."

"Yes. I will send you both to families which are actually descendants of yours."

Yan said, "Great, they are my kind of people."

"You had to say that."

"No harm intended."

"It will be just as before. Only this time you have a mission."

"We will try not to fail You."

"I don't think you know how to fail Me."

"Thank you, Goodbye."

The couple were born only weeks apart. Just as in their previous lives as beings they grew up together. When it was time for them to marry, they did. But before the marriage took place the Father sent an angel to Yin reminding her of her purpose there.

"Your child will come to be a great spirit. You and your husband are to instill the child with loyalty to a conscience that will bring the spirit to the Father's world, and also you must show the child how to inspire others to choose the Father's ways. Will you accept this responsibility?"

"Yes."

Soon after the visit, the woman became pregnant. As in their previous lives the couple was considered special people. Everyone knew their child would be special. Soon their son came. The family was not prominent, but they would have it no other way.

"How do we give this child what he needs to do, what he is destined to do?"

"We must teach him the difference of the Father's way and Satan's."

"But he must lead others. How do we teach him that?"

"It will come. You teach him right from wrong, about the Father's kingdom and he will take it upon himself to bring others to the Father."

The child did exactly that. Before his death, at the hands of those who followed Satan's ways, he showed many people the way to the Father's kingdom. This, a few spirits had done before. He also found a way to perpetuate his work by forming an organization to pass on his teaching. Not only did those in the organization pass on his teachings, they also passed on the memories of the man himself. This gave the spirit an even greater role than he had hoped for. He would, until the time of judgment, be held responsible for the souls of those who adhered to his philosophy. There was no problem with that except that many of those who followed him would not even listen to other philosophies, and this of course preempted the idea of trying to understand others. The Father pointed out that it all was going to work out. If there were many people on parallel lines to the same destination it was not imperative that they realized their situation as long as they remember their principles that allowed them to reach the end. This made the hope of heavenly spirits more energetic. When the world was to come together all spirits would have much to catch up on. Learning about others would be a pleasure.

Yin and Yan returned to the Father's spirit world. They were proud of their son and spent a good deal of time following his organization. As spirits, there was not much they could do. Often times they felt themselves wanting to make those in the organization open themselves to the other saving philosophies so they would understand there were no real conflicts with others' philosophies.

"Your son has done well. I wish all the spirits I've sent could have done so well. His organization will stand the test of time. I only wish his followers could see through their bias and accept others who follow other leaders. I know it won't make a lot of difference in the long run, but perhaps it would be more formidable against Satan if all My spirits were unified. I surely hope that on the last days, the days of judgment, they don't let their bias overcome the principles that will allow them access to this world."

"Of course we share Your sentiments on that subject Father, but that is a grey area for us. Neither of us have even a guess as to Your plan. Of course we're not asking to have You reveal it to us now, but please be aware that we are in the dark when it comes to the matter."

"I truly hope it doesn't create too much stress for you, but the situation will remain the same. It's safer that way. I will say that you two will be here with Me when the time comes. The secrecy is simply a safeguard used to prevent Satan from foiling the plans. Of course the warning you'll have will be the same as the beings will be given. The things that have been told by their prophets will take place. The actual judgment will take some time. The spirits I've sent to bring the beings out of darkness and into My light will go first to screen those who are adhering to My ways from those who have chosen Satan. Any uncommitted soul and those who are found to be abiding according to my ways, I will visit. If I approve, they will at that time receive the blessing that will carry them through the time of separation which I will not describe, again because of the factor of secrecy. I think you'd rather be spared the details anyway."

"Will those who are to be saved be spared the pain of the ordeal?"

"That is a very important point. One in which all of you spirits will be involved. Many of the beings to be saved will lose many of the people in their lives, loved ones, relatives, friends, and so on. All of them will quickly realize a void. For the first time they will be able

to perceive you in spirit form. It will be important that all of you are
there to fill those voids. The beautiful existence I have promised
will take some time to bring about. The despair of that moment may
be an awesome obstacle, if you allow it to overpower the beings
who strove to be with Me. You two have never let Me down. Can I
count on you to organize the spirits here so that My flock is not
tempted to join those who have fallen away? Will you be there for
them then?"

"We are most honored to have the task and yes we do accept it. We
would, as usual, like some time to discuss it between ourselves."

"There's plenty of time. I'd like to add a few things when you come
back."

"We won't be long. Thank You."

The couple was alone.

"What can we say to them? How will we know where they are? It'll
be a new experience for them and us both. How will they react to
us, a strange phenomenon at a time of such acute pain? They will
still have their physical needs and we're spirits ... we can't provide
them. I hope the Father has a plan to get them together."

"What do you think your feelings will be towards the beings we will
be addressing?"

"Well they will be the ones....Yan! They will be the ones! From
that great mass of green slime they will be the ones we've dedicated
our lives to! The ones that have taken eons to come into existence!
The ones who will fill the universe! The ones to know the spirit
world as they do theirs! The ones who live life in the only
acceptable way! The ones who will live without temptation! The
ones to have eternal life with the Father and us! Us! We will have
done it! All the years, all the pain, and finally it will be done."

"I love you."

"I love you!"

"If we can reach them all and convey a smattering of the joy they bring us, we could fill the voids and raise them to a new plateau. The joy will overshadow any pain, and they will be anxious to start new lives with us. I imagine they will be glad for our company, but also they will want to be with other beings."

"We'll have to organize a system of communication so we can bring them together in groups. It shouldn't be difficult."

"What else can we do?"

"Not knowing the details, we'll have to be ready for anything. The most important thing is still to greet them, let them know who they are, and try to convey the joy of the moment."

"First impressions are always important. What would be appropriate?"

"We could ask the Father to give His welcome."

"He may have plans of His own."

"Let's ask Him."

"Ask Me what?"

"How do You do that?"

"It's a trade secret."

"It must be nice."

"What did you want to ask?"

"Do You have plans to greet the spirits soon after the separation?"

"Yes. I'll greet them all. I hope I can intensify the joy of the occasion, but there will be one matter of business I will address immediately. All the beings will be aware of the spirit world, but some will be uncommitted. It's My hope that the new perception will be all that's needed to convince the stragglers to denounce Satan, but all those who are undecided must choose. There won't be any danger but I will be reviewing all who haven't received the saving blessing. I don't anticipate any dissension, but it is a formality they will want to receive."

"We feel there will be two orders of business. First to make all those who have chosen You, feel our presence and the joy of the occasion, then to bring them together in groups to facilitate taking care of their physical needs and to let them know they aren't alone."

"That will be good. I'll hold My address until they have both human and spiritual accompaniment to share the moment. Can you arrange this?"

"Surely, but we need a time."

"Make your plans and hold them. It won't be long, but, of course, I won't be specific."

"We'll be ready soon. Thank You for this opportunity."

The couple spread the word to the other spirits. All were jubilant that soon there would be the world they dreamed of for so long. The speculation and talk abounded. The happenings on the planet were translated as signs of the end. Everyone pointed out that technology had advanced to the point where imagination was no longer bound. The population was close to its limits within the parameters of how the world society chose to use its resources. Sin was rampant. The differences among the religious factions widened. The young could not perceive their society when they would be old. Warfare between nations was widespread. The controlling powers could not clash because it surely would mean the end, and the leaders of those powers, who were so closely aligned with Satan, sensed the real consequences of their actions.

Sensing the end brought new challenges though. The spirits the Father had sent to lead the beings out of darkness tried to bargain for more time in hope that those who had been shown the way and rejected it would sense the end too and quickly change their ways. The Father stood firm. There would be no alteration of the plan to allow those who would accept His ways only because what they had been told would happen, began to happen.

A few tried to plead with the Father to understand just how His plan would work. The only success they had, was the comment that it had all been foretold many times, and that for those who were to be saved and those in the spirit world, it need not be revealed, because they would all "turn their heads" to avoid the evil that would be unleashed.

Then one of the Father's most beloved spirits came to Him pleading and He listened. The spirit pointed out that relatively speaking, there was little war. The people of the great nations were trying to force the governments who represented them to cease the evil relations they had with other governments. Every evil manifestation of government was pointed out, and sincere efforts were being made to align the actions of government with the ways of the Father. The Father was un-saving. He explained to the spirit that Satan was tricky and that hopes to change the world situation by changing the institutions Satan brought forth and controlled, would only be a last ditch effort by Satan to save some ground. The total eradication of Satan from the planet meant exactly that.

He brought up the situation that almost every spirit who was ever a part of the situation on the planet remembers ... the time for dealing with Satan. Satan tried to deal individually with almost every spirit trying to capture another plan that he would later use in his morbid world. The deal starts out with almost nothing at stake against one's spirit, but soon the pot becomes sweeter. Often the deal is closed leaving the impression that great rewards were there for those who would do his work. Of course the rewards never came through, but sometimes spirits were lured to do audacious things. The contract is not binding and the spirit can still choose the ways of the Father, but often Satan uses the contract to blackmail. It takes a strong spirit to renege on Satan and choose the Father when the threats are constantly there.

After so many attempts to sway the Father's mind, all spirits stopped trying and started trying to resolve themselves to the fact that there was to be a separation. For many there was not any problem, for others, especially those who had their beginnings on the planet, there was a deep sense of regret and helplessness as one would expect. Yin and Yan felt the pain more sharply than others.

"Let's talk to the Father again. I feel sick from this anticipation."

"I'm sorry you feel that way, but surely you realized, from that day Yin warned you, that certain life would not be acceptable to Me."

"Yan we've both known since the beginning, that it wouldn't be easy. Think of the flood when we tried before."

"It didn't work then so why should it work now?"

"There are several reasons why it will work this time. I can't explain all, but the one I hope will relieve your anxiety, is that I love these beings. They've come a long way, but they can't overcome the outside element of Satan on their own. They have come as far as they can without alleviating him. What must be done now is unpleasant, but it is a necessary evil. I share your wish, but many of the beings will go with Satan. Think of Me. There's nothing I can think of that's hurt Me more. Seeing My great spirits die at the hand of those following Satan is actually less painful than what is to happen. My spirits came back to Me. The beings or spirits that Satan takes with him, will be lost for a very long time if not forever. I can not control Satan. I do not allow Myself to think of what his world will be like for them. All I can do is to contain him to his world. I don't like it, I haven't from the start. It exists, it will be, but there will be an end to it for you…end of story."

"Is the end really close?"

"Everything is relative. The signs are there. I don't think it will be long now."

"What about me?" A squeaky little voice popped up.

"What about you?" The Father said amusingly.

"You promised me a chance to save the world."

"When was that?"

"A very long time ago."

"Well, you wouldn't stand much of a chance now."

"That's what You said then!"

"Things will work out. Why don't you stay here and help Me?"

"I stayed here to help You until it was convenient for me to be physically manifested and save the world. If it's not convenient now, it'll never be. You promised and I'm going to hold You to it."

"I don't know what to say."

"Say good luck and send me down there. What can it hurt? The worst that could happen would be if I fall prey to Satan, but that won't happen."

"You're sure?"

"I've been thinking about it as long as I can remember. I'll be frustrated and disappointed the rest of my life if I don't try."

"What have you been doing all these years?"

"Watching, listening, and waiting."

"Don't be disappointed if there's not much you can do."

The First Time

"A chance is all I want."

"You'll be the last hope to many."

"I hope I can work it out so that I don't disappoint them."

"Please don't sacrifice yourself trying to save the damned."

"I'll do everything short of that."

"OK then. Are you ready?"

"Yes."

The 'squeaky-voiced' spirit was sent. The signs of the end have become more and more prominent since then. Yet there's still a flicker of hope. Who knows? Perhaps all of us could be spared. There's only one thing though, on his way down to the planet the Father heard:

"Damn it! I forgot to ask Him to place the seal on my forehead! It is too late now. I'll just have to be extra good and hope for the best.

###

Stephen J. Burns, a native Nashvillian in his 50's, wrote this book over fifteen years ago. He was raised in the Catholic Church and holds a BS degree in Accounting from Christian Brothers University in Memphis, Tennessee. Diagnosed schizophrenic at age 15, he has served on the Board of Directors of institutions in which he was interred and has worked for the past thirteen years for the Mental Health Cooperative.

He has been involved with the State-Wide Mental Health Planning Council, the Housing Subcommittee and the Region IV Planning Council, the Tennessee Mental Health Consumers Association and the Alliance for the Mentally Ill. He has completed a stint with the Advisory Council of Tennessee Protection and Advocacy.

Mr. Burns enjoys dining out, soaring, and attending church.

Printed in the United States
71264LV00004B/304-360

9 781933 912530